The Mysterious Chronicles Of OZ

Best Wishes from OZ

Onyx Madsen

The Mysterious Chronicles Of OZ

OR

THE TRAVELS OF OZMA AND THE SAWHORSE

by
Onyx Madden

ILLUSTRATED BY

Noël

INTRODUCTION BY

RAY BOLGER

DENNIS-LANDMAN PUBLISHERS * Santa Monica, California

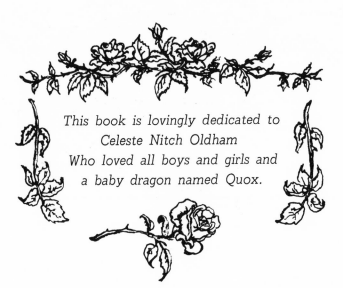

This book is lovingly dedicated to
Celeste Nitch Oldham
Who loved all boys and girls and
a baby dragon named Quox.

Printed in the United States of America
Library of Congress Catalog Card Number: 83-073621
ISBN 0-930422-34-1
First Printing

Exactly at that place where the gold of the day meets the blue of the night lies the Marvelous Land of OZ. And if one should happen to be at this particular place at exactly that fleeting moment between dawn and sunrise that person might catch a glimpse of this fascinating land.

Neither dream nor fantasy is OZ; it is as real a place as you know it to be.

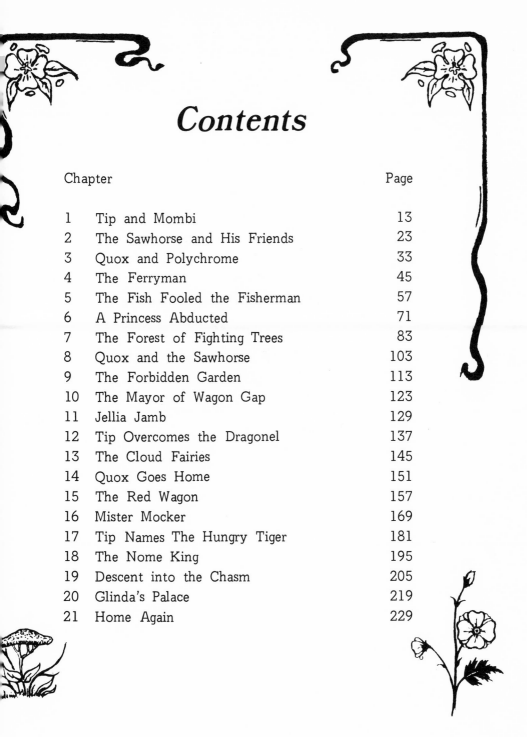

Contents

Introduction

Onyx Madden has written *The Mysterious Chronicles of OZ* and has recaptured the flavor and spirit of L. Frank Baum's books. I truly enjoyed this book and I know others of all ages will enjoy it. For some it will be a journey back to the sun-soaked, dusty country lanes, the cool tree-lined streets and the quiet evenings of the America we remembered. All will find it thought provoking and all will find that Tip's adventures with the Hungry Tiger, the huge dragonel and the daughters of the rainbow provide all the real thrills, humor and excitement anyone can desire.

As to reality, I am asked many times if I think the Land of OZ is real. On this point I agree with Mr. Madden that OZ is neither a dream nor a fantasy. It is as real as you know it to be.

And *I* ought to know. I'm an old Scarecrow of OZ.

Ray Bolger

Chapter 1

Tip and Mombi

As is usual in this delightful land, where it seldom rains this time of year, and where it snows only in the high mountains in the winter, dawn came all dressed in pink and gold, presaging the advent of another sunny spring day. The teasing rays of the newborn sun tiptoed into a bedchamber of ivory and green, explored the room silently and finally, most gently, alighted on the bed. The gold thread of the counterpane reflected the sun's beams, and the emeralds with which it was embroidered glowed with green fire.

The searching little sunbeams danced up the bed, and with playful fingers patted the cheeks, and gently pried open the eyelids of a sleeping girl. The girl stirred and opened her eyes and caught just a glimpse of this animation which instantaneously was transformed into an ordinary, although beautiful, morning. This is Princess Ozma, acknowledged by all to be the most beautiful girl ever to rule a fairyland: and what a fairyland it is!

Tip and Mombi

It is the land of OZ, an oblong shaped country entirely surrounded by the impassable Deadly Desert. OZ is made up of four almost equal sized regions, with a fifth and smaller area located in the exact center. This is called Emerald City. Emerald City is the capital of OZ, and from it, in her magnificent green palace, Princess Ozma rules.

The regions she rules are called: the Land of Purple Mountains, which lies to the north, and is home of the Gillikin people; the Land of Sky Blue Waters, which lies to the east, and is the home of the Munchkins; Rosewood Meadows, the land to the south, and the home of the Quadlings; and the Golden West, home of the Winkies. Each of these provinces is noted for a predominately distinctive color; purple, blue, red and yellow, respectively, and of course green in the case of Emerald City.

Ozma lay in her bed enjoying the morning calm as her thoughts carried her back to other beautiful mornings which had brought with them many strange and wonderful adventures. A slight frown crossed her face as she thought of the many present duties inherent in ruling this land, of her continuing lessons in lady-like carriage and deportment, and of the long gowns and robes of state she customarily wore. These, and other considerations, she felt, kept her from enjoying the freedom of action and adventure she had engaged in as a boy.

For Ozma had indeed been a boy for quite some time. When just a baby, she had been transformed from a girl to a boy who was called Tippetarius. It was only just recently that the enchantment had been broken and Ozma had regained her rightful body.

Ozma's earliest memories were of life in a ratatatati OZ house with the two distinctive OZ chimneys. It was far away in the Land of Purple Mountains. Purple, in all its shades and hues, is not only the predominant color of this section of Oz but is also the favorite one. All the flowers here are purple colored: violets, lilac and loosestrife. Thickets of meadowsweet flourish between the waving stems of valerian and clumps of lupine. The grass, although green, is so thickly interlaced with fescue that when seen from a distance has a purple cast. The great mountains, which give this land its name, also have a purple hue.

The house that Ozma remembered so well belonged to an old woman named Mombi, who if not actually a wicked witch could certainly pass for one. The house was small, consisting of two bedrooms, a living room and a kitchen. Mombi used the kitchen for some of her experiments in magic as well as for cooking meals. This did not improve the tastiness of the food. At the rear of the house was a combination barn and stable which housed, among other animals, Mombi's pride: a four-horned purple colored cow.

Tippetarius, called Tip for short, had been raised by Mombi ever since he was a baby, so he had no real knowledge of who he really was or from where he came. As he grew older, under the not always tender ministrations of Mombi, he often wondered as to his true identity. He knew that Mombi was not his parent for she had told him many times that she was his guardian and for that reason he must obey her. At times he seemed to recollect strange occurances, but when he mentioned these thoughts to Mombi, she insisted that he was only daydreaming and should stop it and do more work around the house. He was a sensitive boy, full of love and compassion, and would have loved even Mombi if she had permitted.

Tip and Mombi

Mombi was a twisted, stooped old woman whose long nose hooked down over her sunken lips. Her long black hair was seldom dressed and when freed from her bonnet fell in greasy plaits to her shoulders. She carried a sturdy gnarled cane to help her as she hobbled about. Her eyes, set deep in her hag-like face, were sly, cruel and treacherous. Even if all her other features had been ordinary, her eyes would have proclaimed her evil nature to anyone who looked into them. Being a domineering tyrant, she took great delight in punishing Tip harshly for his mischievous pranks, and constantly threatened punishment for imaginary misdemeanors. She forbade Tip any contact with strangers and emphasized this cruel order by intimating that if he disobeyed, she would transform him into another shape entirely. Taken altogether, she was a particularly unlovely person.

There was no school in the vicinity, nor were there any children. As a matter of fact there were few neighbors and none in the immediate area. One of the nearest neighbors was Jimb Jamb, who lived almost a half a mile away, along the road toward Emerald City. One might think this lonesome area had been chosen by Mombi for some particular reason, and if one thought this he would be right.

There were two reasons why Mombi wanted to live in such isolation: first, she was an inveterate dabbler in magic and the occult, and for this reason she was feared and mistrusted by others; second, she had promised the Wonderful Wizard of OZ to take the baby 'Tip' and raise him in the most isolated area possible. She had been told that she would be severely punished if she broke any of the terms of this covenant.

Mombi had already received a large quantity of gold and precious stones for having raised the boy, and she had been promised many recipes for enchantments and other diabolical formulae if she continued to carry out this task satisfactorily. And these she wanted greedily.

With the departure of the Wizard from OZ, Mombi's access to his magic, poor as it was in her opinion, was cut off and Mombi was forced to turn to other sources for the paraphernalia she needed. Mombi was constantly afraid that Tip's presence with her would cause speculation about their relationship and thus that her role in the abduction of Ozma would be discovered. So Mombi decided that at some future date she would transform Tip into a marble statue as she had heard the wicked witches had intended. This accomplished, she felt that she would have nothing to fear from them. In the meantime she continued to take care of Tip.

The absence of a school was made up for by Mombi demanding that Tip do certain lessons each afternoon and evening. These lessons were concerned with basics: reading, writing and arithmetic, but certainly did not include access to the special volumes on magic which Mombi kept under lock and key. There were, however, some books on history and geography which the boy devoured avidly, if secretly.

Tip did his lessons, sometimes with ill grace, but generally with good humor because he knew that knowledge was necessary. He was a quiet boy, not prone to defy authority. This is not to say that he was a sissy, for he was not. He was all boy, although somewhat retiring in the presence of the few visitors who came to the Mombi cottage. Many were the times when he had done something considered wrong that he had heard the call, "Tippetarius!" for like all boys, and even some little girls, he was addressed by his formal name only when he was to be punished.

Tip and Mombi

It was a lonely life for a child—hoeing corn, milking cows, cleaning the stables and doing whatever other chores Mombi directed. But there was fun too; chasing butterflies, listening to the soft chirp of grasshoppers, learning various bird calls and sometimes just lying on his back and watching the clouds take their many and varied forms. Sometimes the clouds were like faces, other times like maps of strange and foreign countries, and yet again like castles with long pennants of rack and scud streaming from their towers and battlements.

In spite of all the dire threats and punishments, Tip's natural sense of fun and independence kept bubbling up, and many times found their outlet in tricks on Mombi. Once while walking in the nearby forest, Tip found two small twisted branches that looked almost like the horns of a cow.

Inspiration struck.

Tip took the branches to the stable and soon found out that they could be fitted between the four horns of Bossy—for Bossy, unlike many cows, had four real horns. Tip gilded the branches, for the real horns of the purple cow were gilt, and put them into place. He stepped back, surveyed his work and was pleased.

"This will give old Mombi something to think about for awhile," he announced to himself, then giggling he rushed into the kitchen where Mombi was at work brewing some of her unlawful potions.

He cried out excitedly, "Mombi, come look at Bossy, she has grown two new horns!"

"Don't bother me at this time with your tall tales for this potion must be stirred continually or it will not be effective," said Mombi disagreeably. "And don't tell lies or I will punish you severely."

"Come on! Come look! Come quickly, she really has six horns and you know what that means," Tip urged as he ran from the kitchen.

Mombi knew very well what two additional horns would mean. It would mean not only that she had the only six-horned cow in the entire Land of OZ, but that the additional two horns would cause the milk from

Tip and Mombi

Bossy to be so rich as to be almost pure cream. It is a well known fact that a four-horned cow gives milk twice as rich as the best given from any two-horned cow and that the milk from a six-horned cow is twice as rich again. Also, Mombi thought as she hobbled rapidly toward the byre after Tip, this will make all my neighbors green with envy and jealousy, including, and particularly Jimb Jamb who owned the only other four-horned cow in all the Land of Purple Mountains. She did not take the time to look closely at the cow, for a single glance convinced her that Bossy indeed had two more horns. She careened exultantly out into her front yard.

"A six-horned cow, a six-horned cow, now I have a six-horned cow!" she shrieked excitedly, And as she saw a rare passerby she hobbled to the fence and cried out, "Did you hear me? Now I have a six-horned cow, six horns mind you. The only one in this entire land I will wager, and not only that but it is a purple cow. Think of it! A purple cow with six horns. Come! Come with me! Come and see for yourself and then you can tell Jimb Jamb of my good fortune."

"My good fortune, and I would like to see anyone else benefit from it," muttered the disgusting old woman to herself as she dragged the somewhat unwilling man toward the stable.

"I will raise the price of milk; I'll double it," she thought. "And that family with the two children who need rich milk so desperately, ah, won't I charge them though. I will get their fine fat sow and her piglets or they will get none of my rich milk. And Tip need not think he will get any of it, for I will dilute it for him, but I will drink it, warm and frothy, just as it comes from Bossy."

Mombi and the man entered the byre and sure enough there stood the cow, six horns and all, contentedly chewing her cud.

The man approached the cow, looked closely at it and began to laugh. He laughed until he gasped, gasped until he choked, and choked until he turned almost as purple as the cow.

"What are you laughing at? Don't you dare laugh at me," screamed the wicked old woman. "You stop laughing or you will never get a single drop of this milk to drink."

"A six-horned purple cow, eh?" wheezed the man as he finally caught his breath. "Oh, ho, ho, ho! Why don't you glue six more horns on the beast and then you will have a cow with an even dozen horns. Wait until I tell the others about this piece of trickery. A witch they say you are, eh? No way, you are just a humbug—a fraud—a tricky old woman who wants people to think that she has supernatural powers. Imitation horns and a counterfeit witch." He was still laughing heartily as he left the bewildered Mombi.

A closer inspection of the cow by Mombi revealed the hoax and proved the man was right. So Mombi in her rage pulled off the make-believe horns and kicked the cow mercilessly, even though the poor cow

was not in any way at fault. Then she thought of Tip.

"Tippetarius, you Tippetarius," she called and called. "You just wait until I get my hands on you." Receiving no answer, she went in search of him.

Tip and Mombi

Ozma, relaxed and comfy in her bed, smiled at the memory of this trick and said to herself, "My, she certainly was angry, and I can still remember the lashing I got when I finally came back."

She then threw back the covers, sat up in bed and exclaimed, "I'm tired of being a princess and having to spend all these lovely days handling stuffy matters of state and never having any fun or excitement. I am going to go out and have some more adventures.

"But how can I?" she asked herself. "Jellia Jamb* will have all kinds of objections and even if I should be able to get away, everybody in OZ would recognize me. And I certainly would not be able to have many adventures with a whole retinue of palace officials tagging along."

She considered this problem for a while, then hit upon a solution:

"What if I was to dress up in those clothes I wore when I was Tip. I could then sneak out of the palace without anyone recognizing me, and I could tell people who asked me my name that I was called Tip. That would not be a fib for I have been called Tip. And Glinda the Good would see to it that nothing really bad would happen to the kingdom while I was away."

This was really not as mischievous as it sounds for the Ozians are happy and carefree as a rule and would probably continue to be well-behaved even in Ozma's absence. However, other actions taken by other creatures would cause mischief.

* Jellia Jamb is Ozma's friend, personal maid and confidant.

Chapter 2

The Sawhorse and His Friends

here was one who never closed his eyes, never needed rest, and would never cause mischief for Ozma: the Sawhorse. This remarkable creature had a body fashioned from an oak bough, with a small twig sticking up at one end like a tail. At the other end of the bough were two big knots which served as eyes, and a gash which had been chopped away for a mouth. His legs were four straight lengths of birch, and his ears had been whittled by Ozma just after she had brought the sawhorse to life by means of a magic powder.

The Sawhorse was fanatically loyal and true, and loved Ozma more than life itself. He made his home in the stable adjacent to the royal palace.

The Royal Stable of Oz in no way resembled an ordinary stable. Far from it! This stable, constructed of marble and granite, contained several apartments — no two alike. The Sawhorse's apartment was roomy, clean and airy with a heavy, deep blue carpet on the brown granite floor.

The Sawhorse and His Friends

The color scheme was the Sawhorse's own idea, for he said that an all green apartment made him bilious.

The Sawhorse was a complete individualist and stubbornly accustomed to having his own way, so Ozma merely smiled and shrugged at this departure from the overall color scheme of Emerald City and ordered the reluctant decorators to carry out the Sawhorse's wishes.

They did so with ill grace.

Several tapestries depicting forest scenes, with always a giant oak prominately featured, hung on the brown marble walls. There were several comfortable chairs for visitors who desired to sit, a few tables, a chest of drawers containing Sawhorse's personal items — including several sets of spare gold horseshoes — and a small box with spare legs and ears to replace those which might be broken or damaged. All the furniture was made of oak, profusely decorated with acorns and with designs of trees inlaid into the sides and tops. One peculiarity was that the Sawhorse's quarters had no bedroom — indeed it had no bed. Sawhorse felt it would be frivolous for him, who never slept or even lay down, to have either a bed or a bedroom, and Sawhorse was not frivolous.

Sawhorse's personal attendant, a cheerful Winkie named Bee Zum, had his quarters at the other end of the stable, both so he would not bother Sawhorse and that the late night conferences of Sawhorse and his cronies would not disturb Bee Zum's sleep. The latter reason was really not necessary for when bedtime came Bee Zum turned in and slept like a graven image. Also, Bee Zum's habit of taking several naps during the day caused the Sawhorse to state wryly, that in his opinion the man had been born tired and had never got rested. But in spite of Bee Zum's somnolent habits and the Sawhorse's irregular hours the two got along very well together.

The quarters of the Sawhorse was a favorite meeting place for a coterie of strange creatures who had no need for sleep. It was not at all unusual for the Scarecrow, Jack Pumpkinhead, and even the Tin Woodman — if he were visiting Emerald City — to gather together here for companion-

ship after the flesh and blood creatures had been tucked into bed for the night.

But now the night had passed and the Sawhorse prepared to greet the rising sun. These preparations were not difficult as the Sawhorse, being made of wood, had no need to wash himself or even comb his hair. When he wanted to go out in the morning, or at any time for that matter, he merely walked out.

"There are many good things about being made of wood," the Sawhorse reflected. "I don't have to go to bed at night, I don't have to bother about getting dressed in the morning.

"I was telling the Scarecrow only last night in these very quarters that, while I don't downgrade straw, I must say that it is flimsy and subject to fire. It would take a strong, determined man with an axe to harm me, and he would have to catch me first. As for catching me — well, I am a pretty fast runner when I want to run."

Both the Scarecrow and Jack Pumpkinhead, who was also present, had listened with varying attitudes to these remarks of the Sawhorse. The Scarecrow shuddered when the Sawhorse mentioned fire. Jack Pumpkinhead, with his frail wooden body and ripe, carved pumpkin for a head, was also very much afraid of fire and therefore changed the subject immediately.

"Let's not talk about fire," pleaded the Pumpkinhead nervously. "There are many other nicer things to talk about and do. We might even play quoits."

The Sawhorse and His Friends

"Play quoits at night?" chided the Scarecrow, "come now Jack, it is not only too dark but we would probably make so much noise that we would awaken our sleeping friends. We might even awaken Bee Zum."

"I doubt that very much," chuckled the Sawhorse. "It would take an earthquake to wake him up. He sleeps as soundly as the Soldier with the Green Whiskers."

"It would not take that much to wake up Ozma or Jellia Jamb," said the Scarecrow, "so let's just talk. Do you remember our first meeting? That was the time I taught Jack to play quoits."

"I do not remember much about the two of you meeting for the first time, since I was told to stay in the hall while the Soldier with the Green Whiskers brought Jack into the throne room," remarked the Sawhorse drily. "So please fill me in on the details."

So the Scarecrow, with many interruptions by Jack Pumpkinhead, told the story of his and Jack's first meeting in Emerald City. The meeting had occurred during the time the Scarecrow was acting as King of OZ.*

Escorted by the Soldier with the Green Whiskers, Jack Pumpkinhead was ushered into the presence of the Scarecrow. After regarding each other with wonder for a little time, the Scarecrow asked Jack who he was and from where he came.

Jack, being somewhat awed at the splendor of the royal palace, was not listening closely to the Scarecrow's words. Therefore, he answered by saying that he did not understand what the Scarecrow had said. He told the Scarecrow that, being a foreigner — a Gillikin from the Land of Purple Mountains — he could hardly be expected to understand the language spoken in Emerald City. The Scarecrow was convinced and decided that an interpreter was needed.

So the Scarecrow, whose "bran new" brains — given him by the Wonderful Wizard of OZ**— apparently not in the best working order that day, sent for a little Gillikin maid named Jellia Jamb,† to interpret for them, and when she arrived he explained the situation to her. The fact

* For other adventures of these three, see *The Marvelous Land of OZ* by L. Frank Baum.
** See *The Wonderful Wizard of OZ* by L. Frank Baum.   † ibid

that he and Jack Pumpkinhead were able to understand perfectly well what each other was saying was seemingly overlooked by the Scarecrow, and of course by Jack. Jellia Jamb saw at once that the two were able to understand each other and thought the situation to be hilarious, but, being full of fun and mischief, agreed to interpret for them.

Actually she did no such thing. When either the Scarecrow or Jack asked or answered a question, Jellia said that they had said something entirely different. When she had thoroughly mixed them up, and they had asked her why her translations differed from what they had really said, she laughingly explained to them that, as there was only one language spoken in all OZ, of course they could understand each other.

The Scarecrow said it was all Jack's fault for not being able to understand pure Ozish when it was spoken, and Jack countered by blaming the entire mix-up on the the Scarecrow's mumbling. The Scarecrow retorted indignantly that he never mumbled and that Jack's apparent inability to hear was the main reason he had called for Jellia Jamb.

"I did not think it was dignified for the King of OZ to have to shout at a person," further explained the Scarecrow.

These exchanges between the two friends were finally stopped by the Sawhorse who remembered a very different girl from the laughing one who had teased the Scarecrow and Jack. There was no laughter about Jellia Jamb the day she had come to the Sawhorse's stable and had begged him to take her to the palace of Glinda the Good.

"I had only known her a few days," the Sawhorse related, "but I liked her very much because after you and Jack Pumpkinhead had finished your talk and had gone outside to play quoits, I was left all alone in the great hall of the palace. I would probably be standing there yet if Jellia had not taken me around to the stable and bade me to make myself at home.

"So when Jellia asked me to take her to Glinda's palace in the country of the Quadlings, because she had some very important and confidential news for Glinda, I could not refuse. I did not know where

The Sawhorse and His Friends

Rosewood Meadows was, let alone where Glinda's palace was, but I told Jellia Jamb to climb upon my back, hold onto the stake and tell me which way to go. She did, and we went!

"We had no problem getting out of the palace grounds, but the only Emerald City gate which was open was the one which led to the Land of Purple Mountains, but out we went. I turned south, skirted Emerald City and ran. We passed to the left of Lake Quad, as Jellia called it, and entered Rosewood Meadows before I stopped running.

"Poor little girl, she was almost shaken to pieces, but she was determined to keep on. If she had not been so chubby I do not think she could have stood the rest of the trip."

"You had better not ever let her hear you call her chubby if you want to stay friends with her," remarked the Scarecrow wisely.

"That is right," waggled Jack Pumpkinhead. "And she had better never learn that you think she is plump either."

"Anyhow, I only allowed her to rest for a moment and then I started to run again. She clung to my back as a burr and directed me toward Glinda's palace. We by-passed several forests, a couple of towns, went around a low range of hills and finally arrived at Glinda's. That trip was in record speed, I'll tell you," concluded the Sawhorse.

The Sawhorse and His Friends

"What was she in such a hurry to tell Glinda?" asked Jack.

"It had something to do with Ozma's later transformation. I mean Tip's changing into Ozma. You should remember — you were there — you both were there," stated the Sawhorse.

"Oh yes," said the Scarecrow," "something she told Glinda caused Glinda to search out Mombi. And after Glinda found her, Mombi ran away and Glinda had you chase after her."

"Sawhorse," pleaded Jack Pumpkinhead, "tell me the story again. Was that the fastest you have ever run?"

"Yes," answered the Sawhorse, "I think that was the fastest I have ever run. Glinda had found out what Mombi had done to the baby Ozma, and wanted to force Mombi to break the enchantment. Mombi did not want to do this so she changed herself into a Griffin and ran away from Glinda.

"That Griffin was exceptionally fleet of foot and had more endurance than any other animal I have ever known or heard of," said the Sawhorse. "And with Glinda on my back I was hard put to keep up with it. I never did really catch it you know. I was only able to catch up with it when it tried to run through the deep sands of that little country on the edge of the Deadly Desert, known as Mudge.

"There its feet sank so deep into the sand that it could not run any farther and lay on its side panting, while Glinda captured it and changed it back into Mombi."

"It was on that trip that Glinda removed the stake between your shoulders; the one Ozma, when she was Tip, had driven into your back so Jack would not fall off while riding you, wasn't it?" asked the Scarecrow.

"Yes, she put the stake in the first trip we had ever made to Emerald City. Jack was too crippled to walk," said the Sawhorse.

"Harumph!" snorted Jack Pumpkinhead, "the only reason I was crippled was because you, Sawhorse, had clumsily broken your leg in a gopher hole and Tip was forced to fit one of my legs into you so you would not have to be left behind."

The Sawhorse and His Friends

"Well, in any case, after Glinda caught Mombi," added the Scarecrow, "Tip and one of the girl captains of Glinda's army had to toss you, Sawhorse into the bottom of that remarkable flying contraption called the Gump.* Then Jack, in his usual awkward way, fell into the Gump and all the rest of us piled in on top of him."

"I still don't know what all the hurry was about," exclaimed Jack. "Such rough treatment might have completely ruined my head."

"Glinda was in a hurry to return to Emerald City so she could make Mombi disenchant Tip," exclaimed the Scarecrow. "And what with Mombi squalling, your body thrashing around and your disembodied head crying out, there was chaos. Finally Glinda lost her patience, and pitching her voice exactly on that half-note she uses to command attention – I call it her lion tamer's voice – she ordered everyone quiet. Obedience was instantaneous and the Gump flew back to Emerald City without further incident.

"But that was not the end," continued the Scarecrow, addressing Jack, "when the Gump landed and we pulled you and Sawhorse out, we found your body floundering around, headless, while your head had become firmly fixed onto the stake in Sawhorse's back. I will never

* See *The Marvelous Land of OZ* by L. Frank Baum.

31

forget Sawhorse running in circles trying to dislodge your head while your head was screaming to be taken off," chuckled the Scarecrow.

"Anyway," he went on, "when Glinda saw the trouble the stake in Sawhorse's back was causing, she solved the problem by repeating a magical incantation which caused the stake to disappear and the hole between his shoulders to be filled in. The only thing wrong with this action was that when the stake disappeared your pumpkinhead flew into the air and would have been smashed if Tip had not caught it before it hit the ground. If it had not been for his quick thinking, Jack, you might have lost your head forever."

Jack Pumpkinhead shuddered.

"Sometimes I wonder if that would have been so bad." muttered the Sawhorse.

"Everything turned out all right," continued the Scarecrow, paying no attention to the Sawhorse. "Tip became Ozma, Jack regained his head, and you, Sawhorse, became your original self again, except for your stub tail."

"I don't mind the short tail very much, I am not vain. I can't turn my head around far enough to see where my tail should be anyway," answered the Sawhorse philosophically.

As the sky now was passing through the amazing transformation from the deep blue of the night to the delicate violet twilight which heralds the coming of dawn in OZ, the three friends parted. The Sawhorse smiled to himself as he heard the Scarecrow twitting Jack about losing his head.

Then he stepped out into the stillness of the morning, looked about and wondered what was going on in other places.

Chapter 3

Quox and Polychrome

n one of those other places, The Empire of the Fairy Fellowship, a very significant action was beginning to take shape: Quox was feeling kittenish. And when a fire-breathing dragonel almost a city block long and as wide as a street feels kittenish, everyone in the vicinity should be prepared for the worst. And if the dragonel is Quox, whose mother still called him her "baby dragonette" and whose great, great, great grandfather, Skanderbeg, called him "that noisy little pest," people in the vicinity should be particularly alert.

"That noisy little pest," however, came from a very old and highly respected family of dragons, a family whose lineage reached back far into the misty recesses of time. Quox's very ancient ancestors were the so-called dinosaurs who disappeared many millions of years before even the first of the fairies appeared.

As dragons are now mostly found only in the meso terra-lunar regions, outsiders, who are not familiar with true dragon terminology,

refer to both dragonettes and dragonels as dragons. When very young, dragons are noted for having long, heavy hind legs and short rather feeble front ones, and walk on two legs. In adolescence the front legs become larger and stronger and the dragon scuttles about on all fours. At maturity the front legs again shorten, wings develop and the true dragon, much smaller now than in adolescence, has emerged.

Dragons develop very slowly and Quox was no exception. His child-hood would cover a period of about 2,500 years, during which time he would grow from a tiny dragonette – just out of the egg – into a dragonel about 300 feet long and weighing some fifty tons. After another 2,000 years or so he would reach maturity, but would have become smaller and lighter in the process. His wings would have grown long and strong enough to carry this still tremendously large body through the air.

Dragons, while relatively slow and clumsy on land, are fast and graceful in the air. All dragons are beautifully marked: some having brilliant green bodies with golden scales, and others having sky-blue colored bodies with silver scales.

Early in the morning some rain had fallen and had dampened both the ground and Quox's spirits, because all dragons dislike cold, damp weather. Now however, it appeared to be turning into a fine sunshiny day as the sun's rays broke through the clouds, warmed the ground, and stirred in Quox a lively playful feeling. Here in Quox's homeland rain was unusual, for the days are as sunny and pleasant as they are in the Land of OZ, for these two countries, although separated by many, many miles, enjoy almost the same climate.

Because the Rain King had gotten too much water in his basin and spilled some over the brim, his brother, the Rainbow King sent his rain-bow to the area. The bow arched across the sky and touched the ground very near the place where Quox was bestirring himself. And as always the beautiful Daughters of the Rainbow, led by Polychrome, danced gaily along the arc. These girls are rain fairies, and are the daintiest and most beautiful of all sky fairies.

Quox and Polychrome

By far the daintiest and most beautiful as well as the most reckless, Polychrome, spied Quox and instantly decided to tease him. So the sweetest and merriest of all the Rainbow King's daughters leaned over, tickled Quox's nose, and with a series of *grandes jetes,* danced up the bow and away from danger. Quox sneezed violently and a tremendous sheet of scarlet and green flame, accompanied by a dense cloud of smoke shot from his mouth. As he peered about trying to find who had tickled his nose, Polychrome's sisters climbed farther up the rainbow, and squealing with fear, implored her to come with them and "leave that terrible dragon alone." For although they knew that no rain fairy could be destroyed, they also knew that it would not be much fun to end up in a dragon's stomach.

But Polychrome continued playing, sometimes *pirouetting* high on the rainbow, othertimes *arabesquing* just past Quox's nose causing him to leap high in the air after her. The more she teased, the higher Quox jumped.

Quox would not have intentionally harmed her if he had caught her for most dragons are gentle and good natured. But as a small boy sometimes chases butterflies to their misfortune, Quox chased Polychrome.

As the rainbow began to lift, Polychrome danced down almost to the ground, laughed in Quox's face and executed an *entre chat* which carried her high in the air following the rapidly receding rainbow. Quox also leaped, and at the height of his jump his great jaws closed on Polychrome's robes. Then, just as any terrified girl would do, she called to her sisters for help. They descended in a flash, caught her and held her onto the rainbow, while Quox held onto her robe. Fortunately the gauzy draperies ripped and Quox fell, carrying some of Polychrome's raiment in his mouth. Polychrome and her sisters dissolved in a swirl of color.

After the fashion of young and inexperienced dragonels, Quox had been so completely absorbed in trying to catch Polychrome that he hadn't paid much attention to his own position. Therefore he had not noticed that his last leap carried him directly over the primordial Black Hole.

This Black Hole, the only one in the entire terra-lunar sphere, is unlike those located in other areas. This one is ages old and the intense explosions of energy which formed it have gone out. It has cooled and shrunk with time so that now it resembles nothing so much as a slender dark tunnel, boring its way through space and matter.

In an effort to keep people from either jumping or falling into the tube and possibly injuring themselves, the then ruler of The Empire of the Fairy Fellowship took two actions: first, he forbade anyone to use the tube in any way, and second, to ensure that no one — even inadvertently — would fall into the tube, he set out a garden which completely surrounded the entrance to the Black Hole. He filled this garden with very rare and colorful flowers, and appointed a person named Tubekins to care for the garden and keep would-be trespassers away from the tube. Due to the very peculiar characteristics of the flowers in the garden the ruler also decreed that no one could enter the Forbidden Garden without express permission.

Tubekins maintained a constant watch over the Black Hole and adjacent garden. Always acutely aware of his responsibilities, he had little patience with transgressors, either actual or would-be. He had had several misunderstandings with Quox who had on occasion referred to him as Tubby. This disrespectful term of address was one of the main reasons why he did not like the dragonel, and he spared no pains in showing his dislike.

On this day, as a shadow fell across the plot of ground on which Tubekins was hoeing weeds, he looked up and saw Quox high in the air, leaping after Polychrome. As Tubekins watched, Quox fell off the rainbow and into the Black Hole. He fell in with such a swoosh that Tubekins was almost sucked into the tube with him.

Tubekins, who had been bowled over by the rush of air, indignantly rose, brushed himself off, and muttering to himself that as far as he was concerned Quox's departure was good riddance to bad rubbish. He then made his way to report this occurrance to Tititi-Hoochoo, the Great Djinn, when the grand conclave met later in the morning.

Before making his report to Tititi-Hoochoo, Tubekins knew that he should notify Skanderbeg of his great, great, great grandson's misadventure, so at the next turnoff he entered the grounds of the Original Dragon's lair.

Quox and Polychrome

Skanderbeg's home, which is also the residence of Quox and his mother, was not some crude hut. Quite the contrary. It is a large estate with many rooms, all of enormous size and all fitted with oversized furniture to accomodate the tremendous bulk of the dragons. The main entrance is through a series of porticoes, embellished with carved pillars and surrounded by green lawns and groves. The den to which Tubekins was escorted had walls encrusted with costly marbles and a ceiling held up by beams of moroc wood of exceptional width. There was, however, an all prevading smell of brimstone in this room, which attested to Skanderbeg's usual state of mind.

This time in the den a strong order of salt and pepper could also be detected as Skanderbeg, lord of all creatures, squatted in a mood of rare contentment on a huge couch. In his company was the Unicorn, a pure white, blue eyed, horse-like animal with one twisted ivory horn sprouting from its forehead. The Unicorn is lord of all beasts, as the Phoenix and Tortoise are lords of birds and reptiles, respectively. Neither the Phoenix nor the Tortoise were present at this time, and for this Tubekins was grateful.

Tubekins and Quox agreed on few subjects, but one subject they did agree on was that conversation with the 'Big Four,' as the Dragon, Unicorn, Phoenix and Tortoise were known to some, could be tiring. The 'Big Four' apparently believed that nothing of importance had occurred in the past 50,000 years, and as soon as one finished relating some hoary old anecdote another would immediately make a similar contribution.

Quox had called his illustrious ancestor a stupid old humbug and had referred to his great, great, great grandfather's friends as a group of boring old fossils. While Tubekins did not go that far in describing these creatures, he did agree that discussions with the 'Big Four' could at times become tedious. Tubekins wisely had never mentioned these views of his to anyone.

Tubekins, always uncomfortable in the presence of the Original Dragon, was also in a great hurry to report to the great Djinn. Therefore he merely recounted the bare bones of Quox's actions to Skanderbeg. He watched the old dragon's eyes begin to gleam and his body tense. He heard the heavy rumblings of the dragon's inner fires and noted that the smell of brimstone had begun to replace that of salt and pepper as Skanderbeg's rage grew.

"That idiotic, foolish, unthinking young whipper-snapper of a dragon-el has brought nothing but disgrace to this household and contempt for all dragons ever since his birth!" erupted Skanderbeg.

"He is wild, irresponsible and disrespectful, and if I am not mistaken this is the second time that he has been in trouble in the Forbidden Garden. I told young Tititi-Hoochoo that he should punish Quox severely the first time he was caught in the Forbidden Garden, but the Great Djinn would not listen to me. Now see what has happened. Perhaps this time the ruler of this empire will heed my advice and discipline Quox rigorously, although I doubt it. If I have told my friend the Unicorn once, I have told him a hundred times that our present ruler's attitude toward the punishment of malefactors is entirely too soft and that we will not see justice done until his decisions compare more favorably with those of his predecessors."

As the Unicorn neighed his approval of, and agreement with these sentiments, Tubekins made his way out into the open air and proceeded on toward the Great Djinn's palace.

Quox and Polychrome

The grounds and palace of Tititi-Hoochoo held many wonders to which Tubekins paid not the slightest bit of attention. He strode by a fountain of varied colored fire which erupted and receded with breathtaking magnificence. He passed a flock of gorgeously plumed birds, climbed the marble and malachite stairway and entered the foyer. He continued past beautiful tapestries, woven with strange scenes from no earthly happenings, until he approached a portiere fashioned of crystal spears which almost reached to the floor. This curtain of crystal gave out a shower of multi-colored sparks as he thrust his way through it and approached a large, opaque circular screen. He spoke nine words at the screen in a now almost forgotten tongue.

The screen brightened; blurred shadows and vague sounds sharpened and became more distinct. Something was taking shape. Then, without warning, the screen became three dimensional and Tubekins stepped through it into the throne room of the Great Djinn.

The walls of this room were overlaid with a lacquer of mother-of-pearl whose pinks, blues, greens and yellows blended into an irridescence which defied the eye to single out any of its varied colors. Tititi-Hoochoo rose from a throne adorned with jewels that dripped fire, and walked toward Tubekins.

Tititi-Hoochoo, the Great Djinn, is the ruler of the entire meso terra-lunar sphere, otherwise known as the Empire of the Fairy Fellowship, and is one of the most powerful forces extant. He represents pure reason, and contrary to Skanderbeg's opinion, dispenses justice unadulterated by either sympathy or pity. Although the Great Djinn has no heart, he is considered to be a force of good.

"Thank you for coming to report to me Tubekins," said the Great Djinn graciously, "but I already know what has happened to Quox. He has landed in the Land of OZ. I have learned that Glinda the Good, Royal Sorceress of OZ, is cognizant of this fact, and that the ruler of OZ, a young princess named Ozma, is in the immediate area. Therefore, I do not think that I should attempt to solve the problem of Quox for them, as each of them is very powerful in her own right. Also it is no part of wisdom for anyone to meddle in another's problem for each of us must fulfill his own destiny, Quox included. I will not intervene unless specifically requested. As for Quox, the manner in which he behaves himself in this strange situation will have great bearing on his punishment.

"For sometime now," the Great Djinn continued, half to himself, "I have been planning to send a gift to Princess Ozma, welcoming her as a fellow ruler. When she solves this problem with Quox, as I am certain she will, I will send her the magic picture which hangs in my study. I know that it will prove useful to her and that she will be pleased to receive it for it is the only one of its kind in existence."

Meanwhile poor Quox had been sliding through the absolute darkness of the Black Hole at an ever increasing rate of speed. He had tried to slow his rate of fall by extending his claws but the scratching sound made by them on the slate-like surface had set his teeth on edge and had sent shivers down his spine. So he retracted them and fell freely. His major concern now was what Tititi-Hoochoo's reaction would be to this latest escapade of his, for this was the second time he had entered the confines of the Forbidden Garden without permission. Therefore, he was definitely uneasy and this was unusual for it is well known that dragons are the most philosophical members of the animal kingdom.

These thoughts and worries and concerns were sudddenly interrupted by a flash of daylight as Quox quitted the Black Hole. He found himself arcing high in the air over a great sandy waste and finally coming to ground with a thud that raised a tremendous cloud of red dust.

Quox sighed, closed his eyes, and rested.

Chapter 4

The Ferryman

est was not for Ozma. Action followed thought and she bounded out of bed, raced into her dressing room, and pulled a full suit of boy's clothes from out of the bureau drawer. She pulled on a shirt and a pair of puce colored short pants, which fitted down almost to her knees, and secured her long lavender stockings. Ozma giggled to herself as she pulled the sturdy leather boy's shoes over her tiny feet. The shoes were of course much too big, but an extra pair of socks remedied the situation. Now the travel ensemble was almost complete, with only, still to come, a loose fitting, long sleeved tunic of white and violet which buttoned almost to the throat. She danced over to the full length mirrors in her dressing room and inspected herself.

"Oh, my hair!" she exclaimed as she saw her long tresses floating over her shoulders and down her back. "I must get my cap."

Again she looked and saw looking back at her, framed in a face that could not escape femininity, two eyes — so blue as to be almost purple. Big, clear and lambent, they were warm and kind with a merry twinkle that softened the look of wisdom they held. But there was wisdom there, age-old wisdom with a depth that was unfathonable. There was a hint of a smile behind them, as if their owner knew the secret of life and eternity and was amused by it. Those eyes had learned that trust, like truth is godlike.

Now with her hair tucked securely into a phrygian cap, she decided that even though she still looked rather girlish, she might pass as a Gillikin boy after the dust of travel had settled on her.

"Then," she exclaimed to herself, "I will really look like a boy from the Land of Purple Mountains."

Ozma had worn these clothes, which now did not fit her very well, during most of the time she had been transformed into a boy named Tip. During this time Tip had met with many adventures: he had made Jack Pumpkinhead, brought the Sawhorse to life, met the Scarecrow, the Tin Woodman, and the Woggle-Bug, and had also assembled the Gump. Then, because of Glinda's efforts on her behalf, she had regained her own form and became the ruler of OZ. Now she was determined to set out again in search of adventure, not as Ozma nor as Tip, but as Ozma disguised as Tip.

The Ferryman

As she walked out onto her verandah she felt a compelling urge to return to her room, take a ribbon from the drawer of her chiffonier, and bring it with her on the trip. Being a fairy, and accustomed to the unusual, she obeyed this compulsion without hesitation. Then as the palace still drowsed in the early morning calm she climbed over the rail of the verandah and shinnied down the moroc tree, which shaded both her room and the verandah. Climbing the moroc tree was not difficult because the branches grew out perpendicular to the trunk of the tree from its top almost to the ground.

The sun was already going about its business of making diamonds out of dewdrops as she strutted boyishly through the magnificent gardens surrounding the royal palace of OZ. She threw back her shoulders, thrust out her chest, and began to whistle.

"Tip?" asked a voice questioningly. "Tip," more firmly, and finally, "TIP!" imperatively.

Ozma, wrapped in her own thoughts, failed at first to identify herself as Tip, but this last call registered and the boyish figure stopped, turned and recognized the Sawhorse. She also recognized the complete love, loyalty and devotion that the Sawhorse represented. Ozma returned that love just as fully as she received it from the Sawhorse.

"Sawhorse, I am sorry, I was not thinking. Please forgive me," Ozma said as she knelt down and took the Sawhorse's head in her hands.

"Of course I forgive you Princess, but what happened to you? Have you changed yourself back to a boy?" asked the wooden beast in a wondering tone.

"No, I have just changed clothes. I got so tired of always being all dressed up, practicing to be a lady, studying and dealing with the problems of my people, that I thought I would scream. Not that I do not love them and want to help them," she added, "and as soon as I have one more outing I will be happy to return to being a princess."

"If you are going off to have some adventures, may I come with you?" asked the Sawhorse.

"Certainly, I would love to have you with me but you must remember that I am dressed as a boy, you must call me Tip, and I will refer to myself as Tip, not Ozma."

"As you say "Tip," said the Sawhorse. "Now climb aboard and we will be off like the wind."

She did, and they were.

Down the gravelled walks, through the palace courtyard, and out into Emerald City they raced. They passed through the south gate so fast that the Guardian of the Gate, who had just opened it for traffic, later described their progress as "like a flash and a vanish."

After a time of running at top speed, the Sawhorse slowed and asked the wind-blown, tousled little figure on his back, "Well Tip, how was that, and which way do you want to go from here?"

Breathlessly Tip replied, "Goodness, I had forgotten how fast you can run, and also how hard your back is. Stop and I'll get off and walk for a while. As to where we are going, this is the road to Glinda's palace so we may as well keep to it. As a matter of fact I am glad we came this way for I have a presentiment that there is something going on in the country of the Quadlings that needs looking into. That is why I brought this ribbon."

The Ferryman

After they had walked along the road of yellow brick for several hours, Tip noticed that the landscape, which previously had been almost completely green, was becoming shot with red. The distinctive OZ houses, unique for their two chimneys — one for the kitchen stove and one for the living room fireplace — were becoming fewer and fewer. And in some cases the grainy, green granite block chimneys had given way to chimneys of red brick. The rich earth which nourished the lush grasses of the pastures now also yielded clover with its red seed pods. Mingled with the thick patches of hydrangas alongside the road some azaleas could be seen, and in the shade afforded by some of the small copses, which were appearing more frequently now, purple-red fuchsias were bursting forth in all their glory. From the trees the green jays screamed in an apparent effort to drown out the *chhrr* of the towhee and the songs of the finch and warbler. Also coming into evidence was the five leafed kirmizi, called the Kip by the Quadlings. This magenta colored flower blooms only in the morning, and when the sun reaches its zenith closes its petals until the next morning.

The lack of houses, with the resultant loneliness of the countryside, caused neither of the two wayfarers any concern. It was still a golden morning and the smell of the dust they stirred up was rich and satisfying. Tip's only concern was that he was hungry, and try as he might he could not seem to find either any berry bushes or nut trees.

"Sawhorse," Tip said, "I am awfully hungry. You didn't think to bring any breakfast did you?"

The sawhorse rolled a knotty eye up at his companion and snorted.

After another hour or so of travel, the two came to the bank of a river which flowed eastward out of Lake Quad. Although the river was neither particularly wide or swift, it did present an obstacle to the travelers, and Tip wondered how to cross it without getting wet.

"Come on Tip," said the Sawhorse, "take off your shoes and stockings and climb aboard. This will not be the first time I have carried you across a river. Remember when I carried you across the Gillikin River with Jack Pumpkinhead holding onto my tail? Come on!"

The Ferryman

"Sawhorse, wait a minute. There is a boat tied up to the bank down there with a man sitting alongside it, fishing. I will ask him to take us across," said Tip.

They both set out down stream toward a gaily painted, flat bottomed scow, which lay nosing its blunt bow into the bank. Tip approached the man who was sitting beside the boat, bade him good morning and asked if he would take them across the river.

At Tip's greeting and question the boatman pushed back his hat, laid down his fishing pole and surveyed Tip and the Sawhorse for a long minute. Then he asked, crossly, "Can you pay me for taking you across the river? I am the ferryman here and I do not pole people across the river just for the exercise. Besides I would have to leave off fishing."

"I am sorry, I have nothing to pay you with," Tip answered, "but we would surely appreciate a ride."

Well then, I'll tell you what," rejoined the man slyly, "you can chop some wood for my wife, and if you chop enough we might even include a snack — that is if you are hungry."

The Ferryman

This sounded very good to Tip, who had not had any breakfast and was very hungry. He trotted along in order to keep up with the man's long strides, "How is fishing? Do you ever catch anything?"

The man looked at him narrowly and answered, "Fishing is good here, if you know how to do it. I can catch my share any day I want."

The ferryman was quite rough and lazy as well as dishonest, and he thought by taking advantage of Tip in this way he could force Tip to chop enough wood to satisfy his wife's needs for a week. He knew quite well that it was his duty to ferry people across the river when they so requested, and that it was against the law to demand payment. The man thought that as Tip was only a young boy he might not know this, but he was wrong. Tip did know it, he knew it very well, but decided that he would accept the condition of chopping the wood as a part of his adventure.

As they walked toward the boatman's house, the ferryman asked, "Boy, what is your name and where do you come from? I hope you are not running away from home," he added sententiously.

"Some people call me Tip which is short for Tippetarius, and I am on a vacation from Emerald City. This is my companion, the Sawhorse."

"You certainly have a funny name, almost as funny sounding as that sawhorse is funny looking," said the man, rudely. "Well, you are right on the edge of the Emerald City area. Across the river is the country of the Quadlings, known as Rosewood Meadows."

Tip looked across and saw that the road of yellow brick stopped at the river's edge while another road, made of crushed oyster shell, led off to the south.

The three went around to the woodshed, where the ferryman said, "Here is the axe and there are some logs to be cut. You start chopping and I will go see if my wife is back yet from her berry picking. If she is I'll tell her you are here." And off he went, leaving Tip holding a great big double-bitted axe.

Tip, who had not chopped anything since his transformation, and whose hands were now soft and pink, dragged a large limb into the clearing,

picked up the axe and started
to chop the limb. The axe was
so heavy and the wood so tough
that he hardly dented it with
his first swing. Tip persevered
however, and swung the axe
time after time, but never seemed
to be able to hit twice in the
same place.

The limb began to look as if
it had been chewed, not chopped,
and Tip was almost ready to cry
from frustration and disappoint-
ment. Perspiration was running
into his eyes, his arms were ach-
ing from this unaccustomed
labor, and his hands hurt intense-
ly. Big water blisters had already
formed and others were broken
open, and they stung like fire.

"Gosh," he thought, "my hands certainly have become tender since
I made Jack Pumpkinhead."

Tip smiled in spite of the pain in his hands as he thought of the tall
ungainly wooden form, surmounted by a pumpkin or Jack O'Lantern for a
head that he had made to frighten Mombi. Tip had chopped small branches
to make legs and arms, which had fitted to a body made of tree bark. He
whittled pegs for joints and carved a pumpkin for a head, and Mombi had
brought the creature to life with some magic powder she had obtained from
a crooked magician. When Tip ran away from Mombi, he took Jack Pumpkinhead along with him.

"From the looks of my hands," sighed Tip, "I certainly could not
make anything like that now."

Interrupting Tip's reverie, the boatman returned to check on the amount of wood Tip had chopped, and when he saw the lack of progress Tip had made he flew into a rage.

"Boy, you are a good for nothing if I ever saw one — mooning around instead of working. Don't you know anything about using an axe? I think you do, and that you are just lazy and are pretending not to know so that you will not have to do your job. Well, this will not work with me! You take that hatchet and cut up those smaller pieces for kindling, and don't you dare tell me you can't do that. My wife will be home pretty soon and will want to kindle a fire in the stove, so if you want anything to eat you had better work. Furthermore, just remember that you still want me to take you and that animated log of yours across the river. So get busy!" the boatman said as he went off.

Poor Tip, his hands now raw and blistered, took up the hatchet, and choking back his sobs, began to chop kindling. It was awfully hard, and the blisters and raw places hurt so much that progress was slow indeed. After several minutes had passed and several pieces of wood had been chopped, a shadow fell across Tip and he looked up into the pleasant face of a plump, matronly woman.

As Tip looked up and the woman had a clear view of his face, she gave a start, stared intently into his face for a moment, then in a puzzled tone asked, "Are you really a . . . . . ?" She stopped and then continued, "Little boy, tell me your name and tell me what you are doing here?"

As Tip started to answer her, he put down the hatchet and the woman saw the condition of his hands.

"What have you done to your hands?" she cried out. "You poor dear, you stop chopping at once and come into the house with me so I can put some salve on those blistered hands."

"Hold on a minute, wife!" ordered the ferryman, who had just returned to check on Tip. "I told that boy to chop some logs and he is either too puny or too lazy to do it. Then I told him to cut some kindling for you and he has not even done much of that. He must be taught not to be so shiftless, if he wants to eat. Now, you go on into the house," he told his wife, "and I will settle matters out here."

"You leave that child alone. He cannot do the work you expect of him, and further, you have no right to demand payment for our hospitality," his wife replied. "What you are doing is not right."

"One thing I know is right," Her husband answered, "and that is that I am your husband. Now you do what is right and go into the house as I told you."

His wife obeyed.

"Now you young scut, I'll teach you not to be so lazy, and the next time I tell you to do something, you will do it!" With that the boatman took off his coat and reached down for a switch with which to lash Tip.

The Sawhorse, who had been standing a little distance away watching the passing of these events, now saw that Tip was being threatened by the ferryman. He neighed his rage and ran at once between the two. He crowded Tip back with his body, rolled one knotty eye up viciously at the boatman and stamped his gold shod hoof down on the man's foot as hard as he could. The ferryman howled in pain and hopping on one leg made his way over to a bench alongside the woodshed. There he sat yelling oaths and imprecations at both the Sawhorse and Tip.

Right at this moment, the woman of the house came out onto her porch and motioned Tip to come to her. He came at once and she pressed a loaf of bread and a chunk of cheese into his hands. "Take this," she said, "and go before my husband finds out what I have done, and please accept my apologies for his actions. He really is a good man, deep down, but he has some odd ideas of how young boys should act and be treated. He also has some rather strange ideas about a wife's place in the scheme of things. In your case he was terribly wrong for I can see that you are no ordinary boy — if indeed you are a boy at all.

"My husband has not yet been able to wipe out all his bad conceptions and replace them with good ones. He will be able to do this in time with the help of love and understanding. Not your Sawhorse's type of love, but yours, for I can see in your eyes that you already know one of life's greatest secrets — forgiveness. Now go, but be careful for across the river the road leads to the Hill of the Hammerheads."

Tip smiled through his tears and thanked the woman for her kindness. Then he and the Sawhorse made their way to the edge of the river.

As they came to the bank the Sawhorse growled, "It seems to me that the meanest and most knavish people in all OZ are ferrymen. This one was even nastier than the one we encountered some time ago when you and I and the Pumpkinhead were on our way to Emerald City. If you want, Princess," continued the Sawhorse, "I'll go back and stomp his other foot, for he appears to be one whose pedigree connects with the apes more recently than is usual."

"No thank you, let us go on. But you are brave and thoughtful, Sawhorse, and I appreciate it very much," Tip said, smiling at the Sawhorse's reference to the boatman's antecedents. "And remember not to call me Princess — I am Tip."

Chapter 5

The Fish Fooled The Fisherman

ow we will do what I suggested in the first place," nickered the Sawhorse. "Take off your shoes and stockings and I will carry you across the river."

Tip had his shoes and socks off in a jiffy and in another jiffy the Sawhorse was breasting the waters of the river. The river was neither very wide nor very deep but the current was strong and the Sawhorse was forced to work his legs rapidly to keep from being carried down the river by the current. The Sawhorse's legs are only slender pieces of wood and are not really suitable for swimming, but he persevered.

"Sawhorse, look at the bottom of the river," exclaimed Tip. "It is changing color," And sure enough it was.

The stones in the river bed on one side were nearly all green colored; jade, olivite, and feldspar, with some emeralds scattered around. But as they approached the middle of the stream the green stones began to give away to red colored ones: garnets, carnelians, cinnebar and rubies, whose colors tinged the water with a pinkish hue.

Sure enough, they were entering the country of the Quadlings.

"Instead of admiring the scenery, Tip, you might help me a little by paddling with your hands and feet so we will not be carried too far down stream by the current," the Sawhorse said.

Tip did as requested and they soon reached the far bank.

Here, where the water eddied into a small quiet pool, Tip sat down and washed his feet free of the mud he had gotten on them when he had helped the Sawhorse out of the river. The water in the mainstream tumbled over stones and sand and the sunlight flickered brightly on its rippled surface. Inshore the current was lazier, and fat fish lay drowsing in crystal clear pools, while small fish flashed through the water like sparks of silver.

As Tip bathed his feet in the cool water he distinctly felt something nibbling at his toes. He jerked his feet out of the water, crossed his legs, and peered down into the depths of the pool. He saw nothing, so decided that what he had felt was merely the current nudging his toes. He put his feet back into the water, leaned back on his elbows and listened to the skylarks singing in the pale blue sky. Again came the nibbling, but this time it was accompanied by a good bite.

The Fish Fooled The Fisherman

Out came his feet; he scrambled to his hands and knees, leaned over the water's edge, and looked into its depths. There he saw a large yellow fish lying motionless in the water staring back at him. Before he had time to recover from his surprise, the fish swam to the surface, squirted water right into Tip's eyes and laughed at him.

Tip was astonished at this turn of events. He did not know what to do when a fish suddenly surfaced, squirted water into his face, then laughed at his discomfiture.

The Sawhorse, who had watched this action, trotted over to the edge of the pool, spread his legs and gazed down into the water. He received the same treatment as had Tip, and with a neigh of surprise, scrambled away. He called to Tip to come away with him, at once, and leave the foolish fish alone. Tip agreed and began pulling on his stockings, when...

"Welcome to our sparkling stream and playful pool," said a very deep bactrian voice, "And welcome again. Have you come to share your bread and cheese with me or do you intend to depart without waiting for luncheon and without waiting to be introduced to my friends?"

The Fish Fooled The Fisherman

Tip's eyes flashed over the bank and finally made out, right at the edge of the bank—almost invisible in the clump of reeds—a great, fat dappled-green frog. "Please extend my greetings to that somewhat strange wooden companion of yours," the frog added courteously.

"Good morning," said Tip, politely, "I did not see you when I sat down, so I apologize for not having spoken sooner. My friend, the Sawhorse, also extends his greetings. Don't you Sawhorse?"

"Humph," snorted the Sawhorse, and backed farther away.

Tip smiled at the Sawhorse's response then turned to the frog and asked, "Would you join me for lunch and share my bread and cheese? And would you please tell me how you knew I had any?"

"My lad," expounded the bullfrog, pretentiously, "I know everything that goes on around here. It is my business to know for my name is Rana, and I am the First and Foremost Frog, the Supreme Saviour of the Stream, and the Peerless Protector of the Pool! In answer to your question about my knowledge of the bread and cheese, that information was brought to me by Ripple the Catfish, who, even though a fish, is as curious as any cat.

"When I noted the arrival of you and your companion at the ferryman's house, I mentioned it to Ripple and he immediately swam across the river to find out what was going on. He saw and heard the actions of that dreadful man and then swam back and informed me of them. Although I am not curious by nature, I know that I must have all available information at my claw tips in order to make appropriate judgements. I also know that only a knowledgeable frog is a frog competent to carry out his many duties."

The Fish Fooled The Fisherman

Rana puffed himself up, and sitting back on his long muscular hind legs, basked in the warmth of his own self-esteem. He gazed at Tip for a moment, and asked, "You mentioned luncheon of bread and cheese?"

Tip was hungry too, so he broke off a piece from the cheese the boatman's wife had given him and shared it with the frog.

"How about me?" asked a voice. "I am hungry too, and I am the one who brought the news of your coming so we could all welcome you. I am Ripple the Curious Catfish."

Hearing the voice, Tip again peered into the pool and again got a squirt of water in the face. This time the squirt was accompanied by a gale of laughter.

"Squirting water in a person's face seems to me to be an unusual way to welcome one," observed Tip, wiping his face, "and particularly so if someone is asking for a bit of bread and cheese."

"Come, come my lad, don't be so stuffy," rumbled the frog. "This is their way of showing regard. If the fish did not care for you they would not waste their time teasing you."

"I did not squirt you," said the red and white mottled catfish, "I am not even in the pool. Look, here I am." And sure enough, there he was, long whiskers and all, lying in the sedge – completely out of water.

"Besides," he continued, "Rana is right. Nibbling on your fingers and toes and playing tricks on you is our way of making you welcome. If we did not like you we would not play with you. As a matter of fact, if I did not like you I could touch you and give you quite a heavy electric shock. I will not do that to you of course, but if that ferryman should ever touch me, I would give him a jolt that he would not soon forget. That is the reason I am not afraid of him."

"All that Rana and Ripple say is true," came another voice. "If we have offended you, we apologize for we only meant to be friendly. As for squirting you in the eye, I did that and if you want to get even you may squirt me."

By this time Tip was completely non-plussed and he looked every-

where for the owner of this new voice. Everywhere, that is, except the pool.

"Look in the pool young man, in the pool," thundered Rana. "There you will find Chrys the Golden, the King Fish. Shake fins with him and then give me some more cheese, please."

While Tip broke off another piece of cheese for Rana and Ripple, he looked into the pool and saw the large golden fish, now lying motionless, half out of the water. This was a really beautiful fish, whose gorgeous coloration shaded from a rich gold on his back and sides to a pale yellow gold on his belly. The many black spots which speckled his body served to accentuate his brilliant basic gold. He smiled at Tip with such an engaging smile that Tip could not resist smiling back at him.

"I see that you are serving lunch," said the King Fish, "and although I usually eat only at night I believe that I might like a small piece of that bread I see beside you. Thank you."

"You are welcome," said Tip, and not forgetting his manners, added, "If you have some other friends I would be happy to share my lunch with them if you will call them."

"Please do not fret about calling them, they will be here as soon as they smell the food. Here they come now." And sure enough, led by a sleek silver scaled fish, with red tinged fins, came a whole school of small green-backed sprats.

"All right, all right youngsters, back off! We cannot have you swarming all over this pool," ordered the silver fish.

He turned to Tip and asked, "If you please, would you crumple up a handful of bread and throw it into the water just outside the pool? These tads are well fed but like all youngsters they are always ready for a treat."

Tip complied and watched the waters roil and splash as the young fish pursued the bread crumbs down the river. In a moment they were out of sight and in another moment out of hearing.

Turning his attention from the sprats to those fish in front of him,

The Fish Fooled The Fisherman

Tip observed aloud, but to himself, "This is an extremely interesting adventure. Here we have a catfish, a goldfish, and a silverfish. How is the . . . "

The silver fish interrupted him, and declared hastily, "Please do not call me a silverfish — I am not a silverfish. I am a silver colored fish, and there is a great deal of difference between a silverfish and a silver colored fish I assure you. A silverfish is an insect that eats books and things, while I am a fish and not at all interested in eating books. I am told that books are very often dry and dusty and are not considered to be suitable food for a true water lover. But we have not been properly introduced. My name is Chub. May I ask yours?"

"Some call me Tippetarius, but I prefer the nickname, Tip," said the boy, still rather puzzled about the silver fish's explanation as to his identity. So in order to change the subject, he asked, "I am concerned about you Ripple, is it all right for you to stay out of the water so long?"

"It does not make much difference to me whether I am in the water or out of it, for you see I am not like other fish. I am able to stay out of water for long periods of time because my gills are different from those of other fish. Mine do not collapse when I am out of water and breathing air. I cannot live out of water indefinitely for I must keep my body damp or the skin will parch and crack. Perhaps you have noticed that I do not have scales but rather skin.

The Fish Fooled The Fisherman

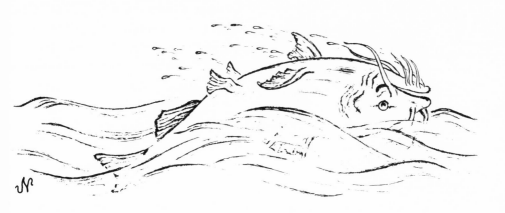

"Now, if I may have another bite of that delicious cheese I will dive back into the river and go find Crusty. You will enjoy meeting him." The word was the deed and with a saucy splash Ripple set out, swimming on his back across the stream.

"Would you look at that!" exclaimed Tip, "Ripple is swimming on his back. I have never seen a fish swim like that before. Does he always swim on his back?" asked Tip.

"No, not always," answered Chrys. "He is doing it now to show off in front of company. But he is good at it, isn't he?"

At this point Rana interrupted, "Tip, I noticed your hands when you gave me that piece of cheese. Did the man across the river do that to you?"

"No, I hurt my hands trying to chop wood. I am not accustomed to using an axe anymore, you see."

"We see all right. We see that the man across the river is up to his old tricks, trying to make someone else do his work for him," stated Chub, "for the less time he has to chop the more time he has to fish, and I do not like that. I am afraid that one of these days Crusty will not be present and one of the sprats will get caught."

"Don't worry about Crusty not being on hand when he is needed. I have never failed you yet, have I?" asked a large fresh water crab, who had just put in an appearance. And what an appearance it was, for Crusty was no small crab with puny pinchers and a faint hearted manner. He measured a full six inches across his crimson carapace, and he walked on ten sturdy legs, two of which terminated in long, strong purplish colored chelae. He waved his chelae, or claws, back and forth in front of himself as he sidled up the mossy bank toward Tip. For a moment Tip was not certain whether the claws were waving as a threat or as a greeting. The crab's eyes, mounted on stalks sprouting from his head, never left Tip's face.

Tip was at a loss to know the proper manner in which to greet this fierce looking crab, so he merely extended a finger of his right hand toward the crab and said hesitantly, "Good morning Crusty, I am very pleased to meet you."

Crusty took Tip's finger in his strong serrated claw and ever so gently shook it and said, "Good morning, young sir, the pleasure of this meeting is all mine." Then he added, "Would you please tell your Sawhorse that I mean no ill will—I would feel more comfortable if either you would introduce us or he would step back just a little."

The Fish Fooled The Fisherman

The Sawhorse was standing a little in front of Tip, with one foreleg ready to stomp on this huge crab if he should harm Tip. Tip laid his hand on the Sawhorse's back and told him that the crab was a friend and should not be harmed. He then introduced the two, but they merely nodded to one another and it was evident that they would not become fast friends. But the Sawhorse relaxed and the crab seemed more at ease.

Rana, who had been a close witness to the tension between the Sawhorse and the crab, rolled his goggle eyes at Tip and said, "Now that we are all well met, let me tell you of the fun we have teasing the ferryman. After what he did to you, I am sure you will enjoy hearing it.

"In the first place the boatman considers himself to be a very remarkable fisherman, notwithstanding the fact that he has never landed a fish. Notice that I say landed, not caught, but landed. He fishes as constantly as his wife allows, and resents mightily any interruptions, such as wood chopping, operating the ferry, or doing general chores around the house. Realizing his passion for this sport, we think it only appropriate that we assist him in every way possible.

"Therefore, every day, and sometimes several times a day, we swim across to his side of the river and take his bait—hook, line and sinker as it were. It is hilarious to watch him when he gets a strike and excitedly begins to reel in his line. Sometimes two or three of us join together to pull on his line. The enthusiasm he develops trying to land, what he thinks is a tremendous fish, is a sight to behold. After we have worn him out and tired ourselves, we leave him and come home. Then you should hear the noise and furor as he pulls in a line with nothing on it. Sometimes the language he uses is positively shocking. And he always blames his equipment—bad line, bad leader, or poorly tied knots. He never seems to understand what is really going on."

"Isn't that dangerous?" Tip asked. "If you get the hook in your mouth won't he be able to pull you in?"

"That is where I come in, Tip," interjected Crusty. "My friends never do this unless I am present. It would be much too dangerous for them."

The Fish Fooled The Fisherman

"All right you two, let me get a word in edgewise," said Chrys the Kingfish. "I want to tell Tip about the time we really fooled our so called fisherman. It happened like this:

"One day when we were all feeling exceptionally light hearted and high spirited we decided to give the ferryman the thrill of his life. So Chub, Ripple and I, with several of our relatives, swam over and took the hook. As a matter of fact I took the hook and gave the line a tremendous tug. This galvanized the ferryman into action and he jumped up and began reeling in. Then Chub and Ripple took hold of me and the three of us began to pull. Now the boatman began to reel in his line in earnest and was slowly pulling the three of us to the surface. Then several of our relatives joined us and we turned the tables and began to pull the boatman into the river.

"Rana, who was watching all this action, says that the ferryman's eyes stuck out like halved onions for he thought he had hooked the granddaddy of all fish. He braced his feet, bent his body back, and began to pull with all his might. He called to his wife that he had caught a whale and that she should come at once and watch him land it. She came with bad grace and that was the very moment when Crusty cut the line with his claw.

"You should have seen what happened. The ferryman went head over heels backwards into a mud puddle, lost his fishing pole in the river and completely ruined his clothes. We laughed for days at the sight of him and also at the tongue lashing his wife gave him for muddying his clothes and for calling her away from her work to watch such a 'ridiculous exhibition.' Now, show Tip your claws, Crusty."

"Look at them closely, Tip," directed the crab. "The chelae are not identical. One is for tearing and the other a holding claw. I am right handed, so to speak, which means that my tearing or cutting claw is on my right front leg, and my holding claw on the left. I have a cousin who is left clawed, left handed I mean. His cutting claw is on his left front leg and his holding claw on the right. But to get back to the game, all that I

69

do when the fish play this game is to wait until the final moment and then cut the line just above the leader. After the fish is free of the line, I hold his mouth steady with my holding claw and pull out the hook with my tearing claw. It is all very simple and effective."

"Doesn't the hook hurt?" asked Tip

"Not at all," answered Chrys. "The membrane of our mouth is very tough and there are few nerves in it. Therefore, pulling out the hook does not hurt us at all, although I strongly suspect that it would hurt the boatman's feelings quite a bit if he knew the tricks we are playing on him."

The sun by now had climbed rather high in the sky and Tip felt that it was time to continue on his adventure. So he bade them all goodbye, wished them all good luck, and asked the frog to apologize to Ripple for him for not being able to wait to say goodbye. All the fish present chorused a clamorous farewell, wished him well on his journey and invited him back again when he could stay longer and they could all have a good swim together.

"So long, youngster, have a good trip. I will give Ripple your message. Behave yourself, and if you should ever need help or advice you can always call on me — Rana the Erudite," said the frog, who was really kind and pleasant, but who could not help being egotistical and pedantic — after the manner of most frogs.

Then the Sawhorse, with Tip aboard, trotted down the riverbank toward the road which led to the south.

On reaching the road, Tip asked, "Please Sawhorse, stop and let me off. I want to walk for a while. You are wonderful and I love you very much but your back is not the most comfortable place on which to sit."

"You did not complain when you really were Tip," retorted the Sawhorse.

"Things were different then," rejoined Tip walking beside the Sawhorse and thinking that the first opportunity he would ask Glinda to invent a magic hatchet which would chop whatever and whenever it was told.

Chapter 6

A Princess Abducted

t about the time Tip arrived at the ferry crossing, Glinda the Good, Sorceress of OZ and true friend and confident of Ozma, was awakened by a cold, moist nose being thrust into her hand. She opened her eyes and saw a gigantic white hound standing beside her bed.

This is the legendary dog that always appears at Glinda's side whenever any stranger, who might pose a threat to her, enters the Land of OZ. These beautiful white hounds, for there are several of them, are well known to those who study fairy lore, and can be recognized at once by their red ears. They are unable to speak, but can growl and bark, and they are savage fighters.

"Well," thought Glinda, "there is a stranger somewhere in the Land of OZ who just might cause some trouble." Aloud, she said to the hound, "Come along with me and I will see what the Great Book of Records has to say about the stranger."

Accompanied by the dog, who would remain with her until she was certain that she was in no danger, Glinda made her way down the hall to her study. In this room, which adjoined her laboratory of magic science, were gathered books, paintings and magnificent sculptures. Comfortable chairs and couches stood on exquisite carpets, which covered portions of the highly polished pink marble floor. Small tables inset with gems of every description held *objects d'arte,* many of which could never have been found except in a land like OZ. In many places the walls of ivory marble, veined with rose, were covered with glorious tapestries depicting scenes of beauty and nobility.

In the exact center of this room is the Great Book of Records, one of the greatest treasures of OZ. Because it is so unusual and of such great consequence it is firmly secured to a massive table by five heavy gold chains fitted with jeweled padlocks – for which only Glinda has the keys. The table in turn is securely bolted to the floor. All important events, which happen either in the Land of Oz or outside it, are inscribed in this book at the moment they occur, and each day Glinda sends any items concerning OZ or related subjects she feels of interest, to Ozma.

Glinda unlocked the book and began to search for entries concerning OZ, which are recorded in red ink. She found this statement:

"Quox, a dragonel from the meso terra-lunar realm of the Great Djinn, has fallen into Rosewood Meadows in the Land of OZ."

Then as Glinda started to close the book another entry caught her eye:

"Princess Ozma of OZ, together with the Sawhorse, has left the Capital."

This item gave pause and she reflected on the possibility of Ozma and the dragonel meeting, and the probable results of that meeting if it should occur.

She dismissed the white hound.

Glinda the Good is not only the wisest and most talented, but also the most beautiful sorceress in existence. Tall and stately, with auburn hair, a complexion like new cream and cheeks which might have been

dusted with pink rose petals, she is no girl in her first tender blossoming. She is a woman! Sure of herself, with a serenity of confidence that no young girl could ever possess. Her snow white flowing robes, thinner than gossamer and embossed with strange and delicate designs, poured gracefully and smoothly along her limbs as she walked to her balcony for her breakfast of strawberries with thick yellow cream, and hot rolls with butter and honey.

Breakfast finished and the table cleared, Glinda tried to puzzle out the reason for Ozma's strange action and wondered if Ozma had confided her plans to anyone.

Jellia Jamb! Ozma might have told her what she intended to do. But then again, she might have left on the spur of the moment and neglected to tell Jellia, or she might have been prevented from telling Jellia. If either of the latter were true Jellia Jamb would be almost hysterical with fear for Ozma's safety, for Jellia was well aware of the dreadful events in Ozma's past. In either case Glinda felt that she should establish communications with Emerald City at once, so she whistled three notes in a minor key and waited expectantly.

In a matter of seconds there was a flutter of wings and three of her most trusted messengers flew in and landed on the arm of her chair. These were ruby-breasted thrushes, good birds and friendly, and of an ancient, long-lived and supersensory breed.

A Princess Abducted

Since time immemorial these birds have been used extensively as couriers and observers by mortals as well as fairies. There is a trick to understanding their language, and if you do not know it you cannot call them to you. Today, this language is known by only a few mortals; however, with diligence it can be learned by almost anyone.

Glinda gave the birds their instructions in plain language. One she told to fly to Emerald City and tell Jellia Jamb of the entry in the Great Book of Records concerning Ozma, but not to mention the statement about the presence of the dragonel. The bird was then to return with Jellia's reply. The other two birds were told to search out Ozma and the Sawhorse and to report back to Glinda when they found them. The birds cocked their bright black eyes at her as they listened closely to these instructions. Then without a sound, they flew off, and Glinda returned to her boudoir.

Here in her boudoir, much concerned, but realizing that she should not directly interfere with Ozma's problems unless specifically asked or ordered, she attempted to compose her mind. While she sat there waiting for news from the thrushes, she remembered a time when she had directly intervened in a problem of Ozma's.

When just a baby, Ozma had been spirited away from her nursery in the capital city of OZ. In spite of the efforts of Glinda and the Good Witch of the North, and with the efforts of many of the private citizens of OZ, baby Ozma could not be found. Glinda, frantic with worry for the safety of the child, searched the Land of OZ to the edges of the Deadly Desert, and sent emissaries to places beyond. But Ozma still could not be found.

Glinda knew that the Land of OZ had been transformed from an ordinary country into the beautiful fairyland it now is in an effort to determine if any country could be successfully governed by a ruler employing only the principles of love, gentleness and understanding. She also knew that Ozma, because of the awesome powers she possessed, had been selected to rule in this manner, and that no other person—no matter how able or willing – could perform this mission.

Glinda was assured in her own mind that the abduction of Ozma was the work of wicked witches, working in concert with the Wizard of OZ. But she could neither prove these suspicions nor find the baby girl. She had had a few meetings with the Wizard, but they were not fruitful. He was reticent and evasive in her presence, but this could have been the result of his fear of her supernatural powers. For the Wonderful Wizard of OZ was only a humbug. The two wicked witches were contacted but refused to meet with Glinda, and such were their powers that she could not force a meeting.

Although a humbug, and probably connected with Ozma's disappearance in some way, such was the Wizard's personality that he was accepted and hailed by the people as a great leader. So, rather than allow OZ to sink into anarchy, Glinda reluctantly gave her approval for Mr. Diggs, the so-called Wonderful Wizard of OZ, to rule the country, for Glinda felt that he would be a better ruler than the Wicked Witches and might later prove to be a rallying point against them.

The Wizard, to give him his due, did accomplish some great things: He caused Emerald City and the royal palace to be built and established it as the capital of OZ; he unified the people under his rule, and instituted several other beneficial innovations. He could not succeed in eradicating evil because he did not have proper access to the powers of good – only Ozma had that access – thus his very presence was contrary to the master plan for OZ. His usurpation of Glinda's regency, during the period of Ozma's infancy, was like the introduction of a foreign substance into a precision gear train. His attempt to rule upset the balance of this delicate, exquisitely intricate machine – the Marvelous Land of OZ.

In reality Glinda's thought that the Wicked Witches of the East and West were implicated in the abduction of Ozma was not too far wrong. These wicked witches had planned to kidnap Ozma, transform her into a marble statue, and keep the Wizard on the throne as a puppet ruler. They intended to allow him to rule until Emerald City had been completed and the people of OZ had become accustomed to the presence and authority of the witches. Then they planned to destroy the Wizard and rule OZ themselves.

These two witches are manifestations of the 'lack of good' lurking in the shadows where light and goodness have not yet penetrated. They are evil. But to think that they have little or no power to do evil is wrong, for in the absence of purity and virtue their dark powers can be enormous.

The Wizard, however, had a different notion. He had no desire either to be destroyed, to allow the wicked witches to rule the country or to see Ozma transformed into a marble statue. But in face of the trememdous powers of wickedness that these two witches commanded, he knew that his meager powers could never overcome them and that his only chance for survival was for him to abduct Ozma before the wicked witches could do so. Then firmly established as ruler of OZ, he felt that he could hold off the witches until, somehow, they could be destroyed. Then he felt that he might be able to make his way back to the world from which he had come.

To this end the Wizard made three visits to the house of an old woman who he had been told possessed some magic powers. She was not nearly as proficient as either the Wicked Witch of the East or the Wicked Witch of the West, but was reportedly able to perform certain transformations and was hungry to learn more magic.

On the way to his first visit, the Wizard said to himself, "If this old creature is as wicked and greedy as I have been told, she is the perfect person for my purposes. First, I must determine if she can really accomplish transformations. If she can and will, I will promise her gold, jewels, and many magic recipes and other diabolical formulae if she will carry out my wishes. I'll pretend that some of my humbug tricks are really only elementary magic and that later I will teach her more difficult incantations. After she performs the transformation, I will have no real worries for I will tell her that if she breaks her promise I will notify the wicked witches of her treachery and they will then destroy both Ozma and her.

A Princess Abducted

An old snake oil salesman like me certainly should be able to fool this old crone."

Conversation with Mombi proved that she could and would enchant Ozma into the body of a boy and raise the boy so that no one, including the boy, would have a clue to his true identity.

On his second visit the Wizard brought the baby Ozma to Mombi and watched as she performed the black magic which transformed the little princess of OZ into a boy. The Wizard left satisfied.

Only once more did the Wizard visit Mombi and Tip, as she called the transformed Ozma. The purpose of this trip was to assure himself that the boy was being taken care of and that no one else suspected the transformation. At that time he said to Mombi that Ozma was much better off as a little boy than as a marble statue, which the wicked witches had planned.

During this visit he also told Mombi that it was dangerous for him to continue to come to see her because if the wicked witches or Glinda found out they might begin to wonder as the purpose of his visits. So he told Mombi that he would place certain magic tools and formulae in a small room in the basement of the royal palace, and that after a certain interval of time she could pick up the equipment at that place.

A Princess Abducted

Over the years there was no news of the kidnapped baby, but Glinda never gave up either hope or the search. She brought all her remarkable mental powers and knowledge of magic into play, but to no avail.

There were others just as concerned as Glinda, who were bringing their remarkable powers to bear in an effort to find Ozma. These were the Wicked Witches of the East and the West, for unless they could be certain that Ozma could never present a threat to them, they could never feel secure in their plans to rule Oz. They realized, as few others did, the tremendous latent power of good Ozma possessed and could use when she became aware of it.

They both suspected strongly that the Wizard had done away with Ozma, but as they were unable to find any clue as to her whereabouts they were afraid to proceed with their plans. Each also suspected the other of independently having something to do with the disappearance for in their malignancy, each expected the other to act as treacherously as she would have done in similar circumstances. But they continued the search by themselves and as unwilling accomplices.

Then the arrival of a little girl from Kansas, Dorothy Gale,* further complicated matters for Glinda. This beautiful little girl, fresh and innocent—yet firm and courageous—destroyed both the Wicked Witch of the East and the Wicked Witch of the West.

* See *The Wonderful Wizard of OZ* by L. Frank Baum.

A Princess Abducted

All the people of OZ, who either knew or had heard of her, loved and idolized Dorothy, not only for her sweet and unassuming manner, but also for having done away with the wicked witches.

However, by destroying the witches, Dorothy had stilled their tongues, and when the Wizard sailed away in his balloon Glinda felt that she had no one left who might lead her to or tell her of the whereabouts of Ozma. Realizing that Dorothy could have had nothing to do with Ozma's disappearance, Glinda explained to Dorothy how the silver slippers Dorothy had taken from the Wicked Witch of the East could carry her home to Kansas.

A Princess Abducted

While Glinda continued both to search for Ozma and watch over the well-being of the people of OZ, fortune in the person of a chubby little Gillikin girl, named Jellia Jamb, intervened.

Jellia Jamb, a maid at the royal palace in Emerald City, had noticed some very suspicious actions on the part of old Mombi, for Mombi was at the royal palace at this time using her magic on behalf of General JinJur, a young woman who was then ruling OZ. Jellia had known of Mombi's reputation for evil back in the Gillikin country, and was therefore highly skeptical of any of Mombi's actions. So when she saw Mombi furtively making her way to a secret room in the depths of the palace, Jellia followed her. After Mombi had gone Jellia entered the room and there found evidence that Mombi had in some way been connected with the disappearance of Ozma. Exactly the degree of Mombi's complicity in this crime Jellia did not know, but she did know that Glinda must be told of this development at once.

This information, plus other clues Glinda obtained, led to the capture of Mombi and forced her to explain her part in Ozma's abduction. Mombi gave a highly colored account of her actions and said, untruthfully, that the only reason she performed the transformation was to save Ozma from the clutches of the wicked witches.

A Princess Abducted

Tip was horrified at this revelation and was extremely reluctant to agree to be transformed back into a girl, but when Glinda pointed out to him that he had been born a girl and was in reality still a girl, in spite of the body he now had, Tip's opposition weakened. Then when Glinda explained that it was Ozma's duty to the people of OZ to be their ruler, agreement was reached.

Glinda smiled to herself as she recalled the manner in which Ozma had been transformed from a boy back to a girl. But her reverie was broken and her smiled erased as she heard the whir of wings as two of her messengers returned.

The first to arrive had returned from Emerald City and he reported that he had found Jellia Jamb almost in hysterics over the disappearance of Ozma, and the message he had delivered had brought small comfort. As a matter of fact she had asked, no demanded, that Glinda send her stork drawn aerial chariot to Emerald City at once and bring her to Glinda's palace.

The second bird told of finding the Sawhorse and a young boy, whom the Sawhorse addressed as Tip, on the Rosewood Meadow's side of Quad River. He also reported having sighted a tremendous dragonel lying sprawled in the midst of some ruined buildings in a village near the Hill of Hammerheads. The dragonel appeared to be asleep for it had not moved during the time the thrush had observed it. Acting on these observations, the one thrush had returned to report to Glinda while the other remained to watch Tip and the Sawhorse as these two set out on the road to the south.

Glinda thanked her birds and dismissed the one who had carried the messages to and from Jellia Jamb. She instructed the other to return to his companion and continue to watch over Tip and the Sawhorse. Glinda, by now, knew that Tip was Ozma and for the time being was safe in the company of the Sawhorse.

Chapter 7

The Forest of Fighting Trees

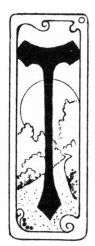he oyster shell road with its tinting of pink nacre led off in a nearly straight line to the south. The road was smooth and hard packed and in many places was bordered with clemantis, the color of whose flowers ranged from maroon to bright red. Crimson shower trees blazed and the petals they dropped mingled their color with that of the Chinese lanterns, which swayed and nodded in the slight breeze that stirred the land. Ragged robins crawled over stumps and rocks, and the leas and meadows were studded with poppies and scattered patches of scarlet salvia.

The two adventurers walked on in silence as Tip looked for and finally found a place to slake his thirst. Water bubbled from a crevice in the rocks beside the road and flowed into a tiny pool, mirroring Tip's face as he bent over to drink. He dipped his hands into the cool clear water and gritted his teeth as the water bit into the blisters. He tucked in a lock of hair, which had escaped the confines of his cap, splashed water over his face and drank his fill.

While he was finishing the last morsels of his bread and cheese, he watched and listened to the little stream as it flowed on, buoying a leaf or piece of bark to some unknown destination, as it raced and eddied past rocks and half sunk branches, leaving some with foamy lace necklaces. It formed other smiling pools in sheltered areas, and continued on its way, gurgling and chuckling to itself. Then Tip, rested, refreshed and smiling, climbed onto the back of the Sawhorse who cantered on down the road.

The countryside was dotted with small woods and coppices. Tall trees lifted their dense foliage to the sky and formed an umbrella of leaves over the road. Through the leaves, rays from the sun dappled the ground and formed puddles of light which seemed to dance as the leaves and branches swayed with the breeze.

Leaving this small wooded area, the two travelers entered a large meadow. At the far end of this meadow Tip could make out the outline of a forest whose trees stood as a dark and frowning wall, barring his passage. He also began to notice a subtle change in the air and ground as well as in the foliage. The sun was still shining brightly, but its warmth seemed muted. The ground was becoming rockier and the flowers were colored in somber magentas and maroons rather than in the gayer pinks and crimsons to which Tip had become accustomed.

Tip shivered in spite of himself as he approached this forest, whose shaggy wilderness of trees and underbrush spread far off to the left and right. At the forest's edge the oyster shell road turned sharply to the right and followed the contour of the forest until it was lost to view.

In front of Tip lay the remains of an older shell road which was now nothing more than a broken trail, pot holed and overgrown with weeds and creeping vines. Along this trail, which curled off into the dark of the woods, was a ruined split rail fence trying unsuccessfully to hold back the underbrush which overran it. The remains of a gate hung loosely on rusted hinges.

Tip dismounted, stepped over the bole of a dead silver birch tree,

approached the gate, and stopped beneath the overhanging boughs of the outer trees. The trunks of these trees were huge and gnarled, their branches twisted and their leaves dark and long. Tip could see nothing wholesome growing at the edge of the wood. There was only fungus and blight and the unpleasant smell of mold.

"Sawhorse," Tip asked in a timid voice, "what shall we do? Shall we take the regular road around the forest or the old one through it?"

His voice reverberated loudly through the oppressive hush of the forest, interrupting the eerie silence. Tip listened and noticed that there was no sound or movement. Nothing but cold unrelenting silence. Even the Sawhorse seemed affected by the quiet and peered intently up the narrow lane which wove in and out of the trees. Only occasionally did a shaft of sunlight gleam through the opening in the branches.

The Sawhorse seemed to be listening and he did not answer Tip's question. Then as if in answer to a command he trotted up the path and disappeared into the forest.

As Tip watched him go he heard a strange sound, a noise like something roaring or braying, not very loud, but penetrating. There seemed to be no meaning to the sound unless it was a warning to someone or something that an intruder had entered the forest. The sound faded away but Tip was unable to shrug off his feeling of imminent danger as he passed through the ruined gate.

The way into the forest was not inviting. It was a dismal, gloomy tunnel formed by great trees bound together by strangling parasitic growths. There was no grass, and a rill trickled feebly over the stony ground. Even the air Tip breathed seemed harsh and void. Some of the trees were yews; dark and somber, with poisonous leaves. They stood like evil sentinels prepared to deal with any intruder. Mingled with these forbidding trees were several small stands of willows. These treacherous, cowardly bullies of the forest, with their upswept branches resembling fright wigs on an ogre, seemed to nod and beckon the unwary into their clutches. They were surrounded with tangled thickets of thorn bushes.

The Forest of Fighting Trees

Tip walked forward and again heard the eerie noise, which now seemed to be a fearful warning not to enter. The noise was coming from the yews, which were indeed the watchmen of this weird woods. As Tip passed by the willows which crowded the lane, they reached out with their talon-like limbs and scratched and clawed at him, and pulled at his clothes and cap. Some alders and sycamores, almost fifty feet in height, stretched down, caught him up and together shook him violently, then held him for the willows to torment. At this point Tip ceased his struggles and addressed the trees with the only type communication that can be used between plants and people:

"Please release me and let me pass in peace for I mean you no harm."

The elm, which understood and respected this universal password of nature, although surprised that this little boy knew the password and language, released him at once and set him gently on the ground.

"We did not know who you were or we would not have treated you as we did," said the elm. "Please accept our apology."

As Tip prepared to accept the elm's apology one of the willows, either in defiance of or unconcern with the niceties of established custom, reached out and scratched his cheek. Tip, who was usually kind and gentle, lost his temper.

"Don't you dare touch me again you nasty, sneaking thing. Whatever is the matter with you trees? Have you lost all your pride and self-respect?" He stared angrily at the willow, which emitted a small but spiteful yellow-green cloud and withdrew its branch. Then, without another look at the willow, and with only a nod to the elm, Tip continued on his way.

After only a short walk, he reached a clearing where some sunlight penetrated the shadows and where a giant oak seemed to hold sway. This magnificent tree, with its great firm trunk and golden leaves, spread its twisted branches into a unique massive crown. But its bark, once smooth and green, was now cracked and scaly gray, and the tree was disfigured by the loss of one major bough. In front of it, gazing into its heights, stood the Sawhorse.

Tip laid his hand gently on the Sawhorse's head, and the Sawhorse said, "Princess, I am sorry that I ran away and left you there alone, but I just had to come here. I do not know why, but something seemed to call me to this very spot.

"Several times in the past you have asked me why I was so quiet, and what was I thinking. I told you each time that I did not know. Now I know! I was trying to remember this place and that great oak tree. I belong here — I came from that tree. Look! There is the remainder of the limb I was cut from.

"I remember now that a woodcutter came into the forest one day and with an axe cut the limb off that oak tree. He peeled back the bark, bored some holes in it and fitted four smaller birch branches into the holes to serve as legs. Then he laughed and said that I would look better

with a mouth, so he chopped a piece out of my head. Then he carried me away to his shack on the edge of the woods.

"This is all I can remember clearly, but I have flashes of memory about being taken from place to place throughout the years, until eventually I came to the Land of Purple Mountains where you found me, brought me back to life and gave me my ears. I am sorry that I ran off but I .."

His voice was drowned out by a deep booming sound coming, it seemed, from the oak. As Tip looked up, the booming ceased and he saw the gnarled old oak addressing him and the Sawhorse by sending out a stream of color of many different shades and hues. The colors stated, somewhat petulantly:

"Here now you two, it is not polite to talk in a language which others present cannot understand. I know who you are," he said, addressing the Sawhorse, "but I do not know your companion. I do know however, that he can communicate in our language because he spoke to the sentry elm. Who are you boy, and what do you want here?" he asked Tip.

"Some call me Tippetarius and my purpose is to help others. And from the looks of this forest it seems that help is needed. I apologize for our rudeness in not including you in our conversation. In the future we will talk in the language you understand," said Tip in the language of color, which is known as Chokiris.

Tip both saw the colors and felt the vibrations by which this language is articulated. He knew that the tree and flowers could sense the colors and feel the vibrations through the delicate feelers located in their bark and peel. This is how all the plants of this remarkable land exchange views and opinions between themselves and with any person who can understand Chokiris.

When people talk they make noise; their vocal cords make vibrations. When plants talk, they cannot make sound vibrations as they are without mouths, vocal cords or breath. Instead, from their core, or heart, they are able to transmit colors which vibrate on the same frequency as do certain letters in the alphabet. Thus the words and phrases emerge as a small cloud of color vibrating at their predetermined frequencies. Consonants only are colored, vowels are not.

Because there are very few people, even in the Land of Oz, who can understand Chokiris, the oak tree should have realized that Tip was an extraordinary person, and spoken more politely to him. Instead, he daydreamed for a moment about the beauty of this language, when it is properly expressed. The letters "b, d, p, t, and v" are expressed in shades of green, "m, n, and r" in blue hues, and purple and orange stand for other letters. Some familiar words and phrases are only a flash of color. "Please" and "thank you" are communicated by a flash of the eighth color, which is indiscribable to anyone who has not seen it. "Peace" is white. At other times colors are used merely to show moods; the orange color emitted by the elm was an aura of friendship and greeting, while the mustard color given off by the willow was a shamefaced, unfriendly sneer.

Interrupting the oak tree's reverie, Tip said sympathetically, "The Sawhorse told me that he was cut from one of your limbs. Did that hurt you very much?"

"No," replied the oak, "it did not hurt too much for we do not feel pain in the same way people do. But what did hurt was that it was so disfiguring, not to say insulting, to the lord of the forest."

"Sad, so sad," mourned the night jasmine.

Tip looked around at all the great trees which crowded the clearing. Cedars, pines and spruce were there, but their woodsy smell was absent. There were tremendous elms whose once graceful branches and pale green leaves were now scrawny and withered. The silver leaves of ash and birch no longer fluttered in this lonesome quiet. Maple, larch, chestnut and poplar still stood as soldiers, slim and erect, but there was no song of birds in their branches, no rustle of little creatures beneath their limbs, and little warmth from the rays of the sun.

The ground beneath the trees was covered with weeds and underbrush. Hedgerows, which had formed lanes of travel for the small animals who had once lived in the forest, now were twisted, tangled thickets, interspersed with thorn bushes and dead branches. The roots of many of the trees were exposed and the natural fungus of the ash tree had spread to others where it was gradually eating away the bark and young shoots.

"Lord Oak," asked Tip, "what has happened here? Where is your dryad and the hamadryads—where are they? I know that the hamadryads are the caretakers of individual trees, and that, except in the extremely unusual cases, they remain with one certain tree for its lifetime. I also know that the dryad supervises the activities of the hamadryads. I repeat, where is your dryad?"

"Young man," replied the oak sadly, "she left us, deserted us and fled to the forest of Burzee. In our hour of need she and the hamadryads departed and took with them the essence of our life force. They, the hamadryads, sometimes called the spirits of the trees, are the ones who watch over us, prune our branches, cultivate the earth around our roots, comfort us and lend their love and joy to our personalities.

"Now they are gone, and in a few years we also will be gone, for nothing can exist without love and care. This is why our dispositions are so sour. This is why we are so bitter toward all other things that we fight them when they attempt to enter our grounds.

"Just look at me for example," the great oak continued, "A man, for

The Forest of Fighting Trees

no reason at all, came into the forest and cut off my main branch and made that little creature of it. Sometime later, a party of people and animals, and a metal man with a terrible shining axe, entered the forest. He set about with wild abandon to cut off the limbs of some of my companions. These trees that he so brutally mutilated were merely trying to do their duty by barring entrance to this group of people. We strongly suspected them of having hostile intentions toward us, and rightly so it seems. Since then, until you came, no one has been allowed to enter the woods. Few have tried, and none recently. As we grew more lonely and distressed we became more vindictive and began to torment even the birds and animals. They finally deserted us too, as did our dryad and hamadryads."

"Sad, so sad," said the jasmine again, jasmine being the most melancholy of all trees, and seemingly able to talk only in the most joyless manner.

"Yes, this is a sad story indeed," said Tip. "I must call the dryad and ask for her version of what has happened."

He closed his eyes, focused his mind, and summoned the dryad to his presence.

"There is only one person in this land powerful enough to summon me here from Burzee," exclaimed a tall, brown haired, motherly looking woman. "Where is the ruler of OZ?" She looked about for a moment and her eyes lit on Tip and the Sawhorse. "Who are you little boy, and what is this strange creature?" she asked.

"Lady Dryad, I have been known at times to some as Tippetarius, and I desire now to be so known. Please honor my request, for a name is of little importance. What is important is the reason I requested your presence. Please understand and appreciate my deep interest in anything and everything pertaining to Oz.

"This forest is of particular interest to me for it is dying. There are no flowers, no birds, and few if any new buds on the trees. The underbrush and weeds are choking the trees, which no longer seem to want to live. The trees are bitter and cruel and no longer form a haven or home for the small creatures that need shelter. Love is absent from this area and when love is absent coldness creeps in, untidiness is present, and cruelty runs rife. This cannot be allowed to continue. The trees must again be tended and loved so this dismal, unhappy place will become a forest of light and warmth and cheer.

"The Lord Oak has told me a tale of woe, and while I do not believe that he did not tell the truth, I would like to hear your version of what has happened here," said Tip, talking through the strange booming noise he heard coming from the oak.

The Forest of Fighting Trees

Having gotten Tip's attention, the oak said plaintively, "Must I again remind you that it is impolite to converse in a language not understood by all present? Good morning, Lark Ellen. My but you are looking lovely this morning," the oak tree added.

"Good morning, Ilexander," replied the dryad. "I am sorry that I can not return the compliment. You do not look at all well or happy, and your roots are bare again. This is strange for I remember the last thing that you told me and my hamadryads when we were leaving, was how well you intended to do after we were gone."

At this point the oak began to shuffle his roots in evident embarrassment and emitted a heliotrope colored vapour.

"Tippetarius, let us sit down while we talk," said the dryad, and at her words Tip felt something touch the back of his legs. It was a giant toadstool, just the right height for sitting, and with just the right degree of soft firmness to be comfortable.

"Now, let me explain to you what actually occurred in this forest and why we were forced to leave," continued Lark Ellen. "Many years ago a man with an axe came and chopped off the . . . "

"I have already told the lad about that," interjected the oak.

"Very well then, I suppose that you have also told him about all the other times you and your trees set upon innocent people who were walking through the woods, and scratched and pinched them and tore their clothing. I suppose you also told Tippetarius about the time you attacked that gentle and unselfish young girl who destroyed two wicked witches thus releasing all OZ from their evil influences. I presume that the size and ferocity of her and her companions has been exaggerated by you in the telling so that it is almost unrecognizable."

At this point Tip interrupted, "I know that story. The Tin Woodman told me that he, Dorothy, her dog Toto, and the Scarecrow had entered the woods on their way to see Glinda the Good. They were so viciously attacked by a tree that Tin Woodman was forced to cut off one or two of its limbs in order to protect Dorothy and Toto from harm. I believe the

Tin Woodman because I know that the Wizard of Oz gave him such a sympathetic heart that he could not do anything cruel to anyone. Even at the time the Tinman told me of the incident he was still so affected by the thought of the pain he had inflicted on the tree that he cried until his jaws rusted tightly shut."

Being rusted was not a new experience for the Tin Woodman, because after the Wicked Witch of the East had enchanted his axe, causing him to cut off both his legs and arms, as well as his head and torso, he had to replace them with tin. This was all well and good until he was caught in a sudden shower, which rusted his joints tight. Dorothy rescued him and took him with her to Emerald City, whereupon the Wizard gave him that which he desired most — a kind and loving heart.

"There now, you see, I did not harm anyone," exclaimed the oak. "It was that great big silver birch that has since died and . . ."

"Oh Ilexander, be quiet!" commanded the dryad. "You are the lord of this forest and you are responsible for what the other trees do, particularly when they act according to your wishes. Stop trying to shift the blame on others."

Lark Ellen turned to Tip and said, "The Tin Woodman's version is correct. I and my hamadryads were here and tried to stop this outrageous act of terrorism."

The Forest of Fighting Trees

Now she addressed the oak, "But you would not listen then, nor would you listen later. All we asked was that you forgive the loss of your limb and turn from hate to love and kindness. Instead you turned all the trees against their hamadryads, you flouted my love for you and my authority over this forest. You became more and more disagreeable. When people no longer came here you vented your spleen on the birds and animals until they left.

"Finally you — all you trees — said that you no longer needed, wanted nor loved us and told us to go because you were perfectly able to take care of yourselves. So I lost patience and left, taking all my hamadryads with me. Most of them were crying bitterly because they had to leave their beloved trees who no longer needed or wanted them.

"Tippetarius," Lark Ellen continued, "that is what the trees did, and those were my actions. Until the trees learn to love and forgive we will not return."

Here the giant oak began to rustle his leaves, and a noise, as if he was clearing his throat, came from him. Color began to flow, but Tip interrupted:

"Lord Ilexander, I must speak to the Lady Dryad now. You will please excuse my rudeness in interrupting you.

"Lady Lark Ellen," Tip continued, still communicating in Chokiris, "thank you for telling me the problems you and the trees have had. I agree wholeheartedly, that the trees — particularly the Lord Oak — must learn to forgive. I also sincerely agree with you that they must learn to love, not hate."

The dryad smiled and nodded her head in agreement with Tip's remarks.

"It appears to me," Tip continued, "that your responsibility is to ensure the general well-being of this stand of trees. This should be done not only for their sake but for the sake of all they serve. The birds and the animals need a viable forest for their happiness and well-being, and people should be allowed to enjoy the restful beauty of the forest.

The Forest of Fighting Trees

"Therefore, if you, Lady Dryad, are to fulfill your obligation of helping form and maintain a serene and appealing forest, you must teach, among other things, love and forgiveness. You must raise the consciousness of these trees to your level—you must never descend to theirs. Yours is an awesome responsibility. You must teach love, forgiveness and gentleness by example. Your proper place, and the place of all the hamadryads, is here in OZ with these trees. They want you, need you and love you. They all miss you terribly. They will respond, I know, to your patient example."

In the hush of expectancy which gripped all things at the clearing, Tip continued, "It seems that the main reason for your departure was because the trees, led by the Lord Oak, would not forgive the transgressions against them. Did you think to teach Ilexander and the other trees forgiveness by not forgiving them? From those bitter experiences all the trees lost the love and gentleness which is endemic of trees. Did you think to teach them love and gentleness by deserting them? I think not."

By now all the trees around the clearing had bent forward to make out Tip's remarks, and they nodded their branches in agreement.

"It seems to me," Tip went on, "that unless you forgive Ilexander and love him again, you can never expect either him or the other trees even to want to try to practice love and forgiveness. He is lonesome and unhappy now, as are all the others, and all they want and need is your tenderness and care. If you will call back your hamadryads and together give the trees this tenderness and care, you will find that their love and understanding will follow. And, when this occurs, can forgiveness be far behind?"

The Forest of Fighting Trees

Lark Ellen looked long and deep into Tip's purple eyes.

"Excuse me," a large walnut tree remarked, "I for one desire more than anything that my hamadryad return to me. I know that I speak for all the other walnuts, and I believe I speak for all other nut trees. Our fruit is dried and shrivelled. I was tempted to offer this boy some nuts, but then I remembered that they are all too withered and bitter to eat. The way we are existing now is wrong. We must learn to forgive and, which is more difficult, we must learn to forget the past and live for the present and future, in happiness and contentment, as nature intended. I repeat, I want my hamadryad back so that I may love and cherish her as I did in the past. Help me, please!"

There was a chorus of color as all the other trees clamored their agreement.

The dryad was still looking deep into Tip's eyes when the oak rumbled to attract attention. "There seems to be some logic in what the boy says, even though . . ."

The Lady Dryad interrupted, "Ilexander, I love you very much, almost as much as does your hamadryad, and I could love you even more if you were not so stuffy and pompous. I know what you want me to do and I have already done it. And another thing, this 'boy' that you address so disrespectfully is no 'boy' at all. This is Princess Ozma of OZ, the ruler of this entire land and all the people, birds, animals and plants, including oaks. So make your bow and stop putting your root in your mouth."

Ozma shook her head ruefully as she realized that Lark Ellen had penetrated her disguise, but she retained enough composure to acknowledge the bows and curtsies of the trees, and the great oak's pledge of allegiance.

As Lark Ellen spoke, Tip saw indistinct figures, that seemed to resemble young girls, flitting to and fro among the trees. He mentioned this to the dryad and she said that she had, indeed, recalled the hamadryads from Burzee and that they were even now beginning to tend their trees.

"You will find it very difficult to see them clearly, Princess," the dryad said, "because they move so fast about their duties. However, you may from time to time catch a glimpse of one of them out of the corner of your eye. But do not stare for if you try to look directly at one of them you will not be able to see her. Sometimes, very seldom, but sometimes they will appear in full view if they have something to say or a favor to ask of a person. Here comes one now."

And sure enough a hamadryad carefully approached Tip and Lark Ellen. She was just a young girl, slim as an eel, with a freckled face and brown hair done in long plaits. Her face, which was normally happy and smiling, was now set in a pout, and her clear brown eyes wore a troubled look, and she was trembling with indignation. She addressed Lark Ellen and Tip:

"Lady Dryad and Princess, I request permission to speak." Then without waiting for permission, she burst out, "I have just come from my willow, who has been crying because you, Princess, called him a nasty sneak, then you went away before he could say anything to you. I do not think it was right for you to call him those names and make him cry. I do not consider him a sneak, and I do not think it is fair of you to not forgive him for having scratched you. He is sorry, and I think you should forgive him. So there!" she concluded defiantly.

The Forest of Fighting Trees

Tip touched his scratched cheek and then said to the hamadryad, "Please tell me your name," he waited for her answer, "Adriel? Very well Adriel, let us go back to your willow. I want to talk to him."

When they reached the place where the willow stood, Tip said, "Little willow, will you please forgive me for having called you all those bad names if I assure you that I have forgiven you for the scratch, and if I tell you that I love you very much?"

When Tip said this, the willow ceased weeping and sent out such an aura of joy and forgiveness that all the trees wondered. Adriel's face broke into a beautiful smile and she squeezed Tip's hand before she disappeared into the willow.

Now that the trees were happy and the hamadryads hard at work, the forest more cheerful, and the cold and gloom dissipating, Tip and the Sawhorse bade Ilexander and Lark Ellen goodbye.

"Come again," encouraged the great oak, "come anytime Your Majesty. You are always welcome, Princess, and you too, my son."

"Well, said Tip to the Sawhorse as they were leaving the forest, "that was some adventure. What did you think of your parent tree and the other trees,and what of the spirits of the woods?"

"It was very interesting, Princess," replied the Sawhorse, "but now I will have to find something else to think about when I do not care to talk."

"You are an old grouch," said Tip, "but I love you. Oh yes, you must stop calling me Princess now and call me Tip again, for I feel we are due for more adventures. And by the way, don't you think that you would feel better if you had forgiven the ferryman instead of stamping on his toe? Don't you really love him, deep down?" Tip asked impishly.

"Humph," grunted the Sawhorse as he set off down the road.

Chapter 8

Quox and The Sawhorse

hey traveled along the oyster shell road for nearly an hour in silence, each wrapped in his own thoughts. The Sawhorse was thinking of his oak and their mutual dryad, while Tip was pondering past adventures and wondering what lay in store for him. Neither noticed a ruby breasted thrush which seemed to be observing them from an adjacent tree.

The road was in such good condition that travel on it became monotonous and in spite of the uncomfortable jogging on the Sawhorse's hard back, Tip almost drowsed off. Then he saw something that roused him: ruts in the road which could have been made by wagon wheels. He called this to the Sawhorse's attention, and that worthy replied that he had noticed them some time back. He added testily, that a wagon was just what they needed because then he could pull the princess in style and comfort. He was still a bit annoyed about Tip's remark concerning his uncomfortable back.

Quox and The Sawhorse

Tip sensed this and said, "Sawhorse, look! The ruts follow the left branch of the road. Let's follow them. I would like to learn whether wagons are made near here, and if they are I will take your advice, you sweet Sawhorse, and try to get one."

The Sawhorse grunted and turned onto the left fork of the road, which led to a low hill. This, the Sawhorse climbed without difficulty and followed the road past some scattered houses toward a small village tucked in a swale.

Ordinarily this village lay somnolent in the warm sunshine, with its people moving quietly and without haste, and the road on which Tip and the Sawhorse traveled was also its main street.

On this street stood the dominant meeting house – proud possessor of two stories. Flanking the meeting house, and on both sides of the street, were some twenty old-fashioned but comfortable houses. They were all painted in light tones: white, cream or ivory, set off with a red trim. The trim ranged from pink to magenta, as the owner chose. Many were almost hidden by masses of climbing roses and honeysuckle. The town's main street was unpaved, but always neatly raked.

It was a street with no hitching posts, no fireplugs, no telephone poles, no parking meters and surely no automobiles. At times a gaggle of geese waddled lazily across the street – seeking the waters of a creek adjacent to the village. Or again a stray pig meandered along it, or a boy drove his cow to or from pasture. Wives and mothers sat on doorsteps and gossiped or tended small kitchen gardens while their bread cooled. But today was not an ordinary day.

The village was wide awake. The geese had fled, as had the pigs, and the people were gathered in groups where they were talking and gesticulating excitedly. Tip rode in and watched all this activity, wonderingly. Then, as he approached the meeting house and turned the corner, he stared in amazement as he saw the reason for all this excitement. There, directly in front of him, crouched the biggest dragon ever seen or imagined by him. It was sprawled right in the middle of the road. It was

Quox and The Sawhorse

immense and looked even bigger, because part of its body still lay in the ruins of some buildings.

"What is it?" asked the Sawhorse, stopping so fast that he pitched Tip over his head.

"That must be the biggest dragon in all the world," answered Tip as he scrambled to his feet. "Be careful, don't go too near him."

"Humph," retorted the Sawhorse, "I'm not afraid of any lizard, no matter how big he is. Come on, Tip, let's move him out of the way."

"Wait," called Tip, "Stop! He's too big." But the Sawhorse merely shook his head petulantly, and walked right up to the dragon.

"You are in our way. Move!" ordered the Sawhorse in his usual irascible tone.

The dragonel stirred and slowly opened his eyes — eyes that were as big as windows in an office building, and as gray and cold as slate. He looked at the Sawhorse in astonishment. No one had ever spoken to him like that before. Then as he began slowly to formulate a reply, for all dragons are notoriously slow in thought and action unless particularly enraged, the Sawhorse said:

"I'm not the most patient creature in the world. When I tell you to move, lizard, MOVE!"

Quox and The Sawhorse

And with that the Sawhorse pranced up and stomped on the dragon's toe as hard as he could.

Stung by the pain, Quox, for it was indeed Quox, gave a devastating roar of rage and pain. It started as a vast rumbling as if an old volcano had made up its mind to erupt, and ended in a shriek that almost deafened Tip. From Quox's huge mouth, lined with teeth as long and sharp as daggers, shot a jet of flame that completely enveloped the Sawhorse and shrivelled the grass for many feet. The stench of brimstone, which lay heavy on his breath, almost strangled Tip. Quox's reflex to the pain in his toe threw the Sawhorse many feet away and shook the ground as an earth-quake. Some trees were felled, more houses damaged and even the sur-rounding hills shaken. And then Quox rose up on all fours legs and started for the Sawhorse, who was ineffectively struggling to regain his feet.

When Tip, who had been thrown to the ground by this violent demonstration, saw the dragonel charging toward the Sawhorse, he scram-bled to his feet and ran right into the path of this gigantic monster.

"Stop right there, you naughty dragon!" he cried out. "You stop picking on that poor little Sawhorse. Aren't you ashamed of yourself? If you are not you should be, and if you do not want to get into more trouble than you can imagine, YOU STOP RIGHT THERE!"

With that remark Tip ran over to where the Sawhorse was lying on his back, vainly wriggling his legs in an effort to get up. The Sawhorse has no joints in his legs and is virtually helpless when upside down. Tip set him upright and they both moved back out of danger, for Tip in particular had been in real danger and it was very, very brave of him to confront a dragon in such a manner.

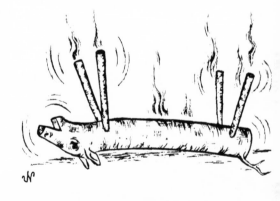

Quox and The Sawhorse

In the meantime Quox was beside himself with fury. To be called a lizard—the worse insult a dragon could suffer—and to have one's toes stomped on by an impudent sawhorse was bad enough, but to be defied, and faced down, by a boy in short pants, and a delicate looking boy at that, was the topper.

"I will burn them both up, raze the town and desolate the country-side," Quox raged to himself.

But a sobering thought came to him: What would the Great Djinn, Tititi-Hoochoo, think of such a rampage, particularly in view of the fact that Quox had not only entered the Forbidden Garden for the second time, but this time had actually fallen into the Black Hole. It might be better in the long run to remain on his best behavior and consider events as they occurred.

So Quox stopped short, sighed and squatted down on the road. Un-fortunately, his sigh was accompanied by a sheet of flame which extended just far enough to re-ignite the Sawhorse and singe Tip's clothing and begrime his face.

Quox and The Sawhorse

As Tip and the Sawhorse backed farther away from the dragonel, Tip looked about him and saw that most of the inhabitants of the village had watched his encounter with Quox from the windows of their homes and stores. Almost in a panic, they had sought the refuge of buildings when the Sawhorse had addressed Quox so defiantly. But as the massive dragonel now seemed quiescent, curiosity overcame fear and the local people began to leave their places of safety and stream into the street. There was still hesitancy on the part of some, but most crowded around Tip and the Sawhorse, smiling and greeting them in a most friendly fashion. Several men, who had stayed outdoors during Tip's confrontation with Quox, were helping Tip take off his smoldering coat and were slapping out the sparks on the Sawhorse.

"You were very brave to beard that dragon as you did," one man said, "and very quick-witted too. You certainly saved your Sawhorse, and you most certainly stared that dragon down. You were lucky, though, that he did not bite you, or even worse."

Tip, still devoured with curiosity about the dragonel, thanked the men for helping him and the Sawhorse, and while putting his coat back on told them that he was called Tippetarius, or Tip for short, and that he and the Sawhorse were on vacation from Emerald City.

"A vacation is one thing," added Tip, "but such an adventure with such a huge dragonel is something else again."

He then asked one of the men when the dragonel had come and where it had come from.

Before the man could answer, a pompous, bustling, self-important little man pushed his way to Tip's side and announced himself as the mayor of Wagon Gap.

"Well, young man, I see that you are not afraid of dragons. That is fine. Now you are in good company for I am also a stranger to all fear."

The mayor puffed out his chest and looked around as if he expected the audience to applaud.

"This is certainly true, Tip," said one of the men, sarcastically. "The only reason our mayor ran away from here when your Sawhorse defied the dragon was to make sure that all the women and children found a place of safety." The man winked at Tip.

"Here now, Mayor, don't take offense," another man said, "after all we did vote you into office."

The mayor, who looked ready to cry at the first man's sally, now seemed mollified, then asked Tip, "What is that strange creature with you? Unless my eyes completely deceive me it is an animated sawhorse."

"You are right, Mayor," put in one of the men before Tip had a chance to reply. "It is a live sawhorse. We had better tell Dcim Wainwright that we now have a horse to pull that strange red wagon he made."

"All right, that is enough," said the mayor. "The boy asked about the dragon and if you will allow me to get a word in edgewise, I will explain the circumstances to him."

In the quiet that followed the mayor cleared his throat and this is what he described :

The sun had just poked its orange nose over the horizon and awakened the birds to their matins when the people of the village were shaken out of their sound slumbers by a thundering crash which shattered the morning calm. Although some of the people were so frightened that they stayed in bed and pulled the covers over their heads, most ran out of doors to see what in the world had happened. What had happened was epic.

Quox and The Sawhorse

There in the lightness of the mild spring morning, sprawled out on the ruins of several houses, a workshop and two barns, lay a perfectly enormous dragonel. His immense sky-blue body was covered with silver scales the size of serving trays; his legs and feet, ending in claws the size of sabers, were tucked into his sides; his head, with its curiously upturned nose, and a double row of teeth the size of daggers, lay in the road, and his tail, almost half as long as a city block, curled behind him. Wisps of vapour, which bore the unmistakable odor of salt and pepper, drifted from his nostrils, and a heavy bubbling hum, mixed with the sound like a giant tom cat purring, accompanied his breathing.

The odor of salt and pepper which can be detected on the breath of dragons—when they are not angered or showing off—is also a peculiarity of a large flying member of a cadet branch of dragons, the Roc. The dragonel lay motionless, heedless of the cries of the people who were being crushed beneath his vast bulk.

"It was very unnerving," the mayor explained, "but even in the face of such danger some people ran up to the monster to get a better look. As the more daring ones approached his nose a strange thing happened. The dragon raised himself on all four legs and began to raise and lower his body, rhythmically, while his throat and chest began to expand and pulsate. He opened that dreadful mouth and exhaled a sheet of crimson and green flame that seemed to be a hundred feet long. Some of the people were badly burned, but most escaped with a minor singeing. The dragon appeared almost to double his size, and perhaps that was his intent.

"It is possible that he merely wanted to seem to be larger than he actually is in order to frighten any possible enemies away. In any case, when he lifted himself up, the people whom he had been crushing beneath him were able to scramble out and run to safety. Some ran so well that they have not come back yet."

The mayor also told Tip about a man named Dcim Wainwright, who had recently emigrated from the Land of Ev and had made his home here.

"As it is not unusual for a person to be named for the type of work he does," explained the mayor, "Mr. Wainwright is a wagon maker. As a matter of fact he is both a wainwright and a carter. That is because he not only makes wagons and carts, he also drives them when the occasion arises. He is a kind and gentle man who is well liked and respected in the community."

It was this Mr. Wainwright who, when the dust had settled, approached the dragon — timidly to be sure — and addressed the intruder.

"Sir Dragon," said the man respectfully, "my name is Wainwright and I am by trade both a carter and a wagoner. I build these conveyances for . . ."

Quox slowly opened his eyes and interrupted, rather rudely, "Did you say your name was Carter?" he asked coldly.

"No, Your Honor, my name is Wainwright, but I am a carter. I am also a wagon maker, so my name is Wainwright not Carter. But you may call me either Carter or Wainwright, whichever you choose," responded Wainwright.

Quox and The Sawhorse

Quox, a little puzzled by the explanation of these many names and titles, pondered for a moment then asked, "What do you want?"

"Most noble dragon," said Mr. Wainwright, "when you dropped in on us so unexpectedly, although you are very welcome I assure you, you fell on my factory and demolished it. The only article which appears not to have been damaged is a red wagon. It is now standing right next to your tail."

"Well, what about it? Tell me what you want. Don't take all day?" demanded Quox, irritably.

"I was wondering if your eminence would allow me and several of my workman to move the wagon so it would not be damaged by any sudden movement of yours. I would consider it a very great favor," concluded Mr. Wainwright.

Quox, somewhat surprised by this request, stared long and hard at the carter. While he was staring, Quox remembered that he had promised himself to take revenge on anyone he met either named Carter or who was a carter, or who had anything to do with carts or wagons. Now here was a man who fitted this category asking a favor.

The reason for Quox's monumental detestation of carters and wainwrights was an occurrance which had taken place in Quox's homeland, the Empire of the Fairy Fellowship, when he was a baby.

This is the event as Quox remembered it, with Tubekins, as usual, tattling to Titti-Hoochoo.

Chapter 9

The Forbidden Garden

I will have that dragonette's scales if it is the last thing I do," exclaimed Tubekins as he made his way to the Great Djinn's palace. "It seems to me that all I do is complain to Tititi-Hoochoo about the mischief that Quox gets into. Well, this time he has gone too far."

And Quox, indeed, even though he was only a very young and tender dragon, was in deep trouble. He had not only picked the sacred flowers of the sun but had called upon his dragon and damosel flies to destroy the bumble bees, who guarded those flowers.

To pick these flowers, without proper authorization, was one of the worst crimes which could be committed in the land — The Empire of the Fairy Fellowship.

Quox was not a bad dragonette, but after the fashion set by little boys and puppies, he was forever into something or other. This curiosity, coupled with his pre-adolescent clumsiness, made him a distinct menace when he was in the vicinity of anything fragile or expensive. These shortcomings, added to his almost irresistible impulses to act without thinking, made life difficult, not only for Quox, but for his mother, his irascible great, great, great grandfather and almost anyone else who happened to encounter him.

Quox's most recent trouble began several days after his six hundred and fiftieth birthday. On this auspicious occasion, after Quox had been measured and found to be ten feet from the tip of his nose to the tip of his tail, he had received from his mother and his great, great, great grandfather, a brand new bicycle — the very first one he had ever owned. He took to it with relish, and after a few days of bumps and scrapes, and the destruction of some exceedingly fine rare shrubs, had mastered the intricacies of cycling.

On this day as he was riding his bicycle past the Forbidden Gardens, he was struck with a compelling impulse of such magnitude that he almost fell off his bike. He would pick a bouquet of flowers for his mother, both to show his love for her and to thank her for the new bicycle. The thought was the deed with Quox so he stopped, laid down his bike and scuttled over the garden wall. And there in the midst of the beautiful melodies and the fragrant perfume and riotous colors of the flowers, he began to gather his bouquet. Tubekins, the caretaker of both the garden and the Forbidden Tube, was spading industriously, oblivious of Quox's presence.

The Forbidden Garden

The Forbidden Garden is a very unusual garden. It could only be found in a place like Tititi-Hoochoo's meso terra-lunar realm — The Empire of the Fairy Fellowship. All of the flowers which grow here not only have the most brilliant colors and spicy fragrances, but also emit musical tones which, when combined produce the most agreeable chords.

All the flowers in this garden are dedicated to the powers of light, and the sunflowers are particularly sacred to the sun — after whom they are named. As all flowers wilt after they have been picked, it is against the law for any person to pick them without authorization. Also, if they were picked indiscriminately, there would not be enough of them to furnish the beautiful accompaniments for the daily matin and vesper services. On certain festival days, great numbers of flowers are picked and made into bouquets, with much attention being paid to color, fragrance, and tone. When assembled in this manner, lovely musical chords are forthcoming and when enough are properly integrated, superb etudes, fugues and rhapsodies are produced.

The sunflower, with its note like a struck silver bell, is far and away the most stirring. Its tone surpasses even the light airy notes of the hyacinth, the rich mellow ring of the magenta fushia, and the soft cool notes of the tenuibala, and the grand, sonorous tones coming from deep in the trumpet-like flowers of the gentian. Carnations, roses, violets, crysanthemums and cornflowers, all add acceptable tones to the orchestration. All but the snapdragons.

The varicolored, striped snapdragon, with its assortment of tones, is highly regarded but can never be relied upon to produce pure, sustained notes. Due to their stripes and various colors, snapdragons sometimes drift off into discordant sharps and flats. The tones of all these flowers are muted until they are organized into bouquets, wreaths or other floral arrangements. Only then do their tones ring out loud and clear — all but the sunflowers.

Quox was probably unaware that he was committing a crime by

picking the flowers, although to be honest he might not have been deterred if he had known. After all, he was only a dragonette —a baby, so he began to prepare the posey. First, came several fushias, then some hyacinth and tenuibala, some gentian and finally, a border of snapdragons. So far so good, he thought, and if he had been satisfied with this bouquet, he probably would have escaped scot free. But no, the majestic sunflowers, tall and stately, gleaming golden in the sun's warm rays seemed to beckon him as they nodded in the breeze. All Quox could see then, was a great dazzling sunburst of gold lying amid the red, blue, green and purple of the other flowers, the whole set off by the edging of multi-colored snapdragons.

Quox romped over and picked the sunflower.

At the moment he plucked it, it emitted its own unique tone, which rose on the late morning air like a tocsin, freezing Quox and alerting Tubekins. Tubekins, at once, dropped his spade, swung his eyes toward the bed of sunflowers and placed a silver whistle to his lips. As he saw the head of Quox and the sunflower disappearing behind a hedge, he blew his whistle and the guardian bumblebees answered the summons.

The Forbidden Garden

These bumblebees, which had been appointed by Tititi-Hoochoo to guard the flowers in the Forbidden Garden, were certainly a force to be reckoned with. Their bodies, with their black backs, yellow abdomens and faces, and long red stingers, are bigger than a man's thumb. Their thick legs are covered with coarse, dense hair and their wings are exceedingly sturdy. They are easily irritated and when angry pursue their victims and sting them painfully. As watchdogs of the garden they knew what to do to Quox when they sighted him, and proceeded to try to do it.

Quox did not wait around to argue his case either with Tubekins or the bees. Still clutching his melodious bouquet, he made for the wall as fast as his legs would carry him. He trampled everything which stood in his way, much to the chagrin of Tubekins who made his feelings known at the top of his voice. It was at this time that the first of the bees stung Quox, whose shriek of pain added to this most startling cacaphony coming from the garden. And it was right after he was stung that Quox remembered to call upon his friends, the dragonflies, for help.

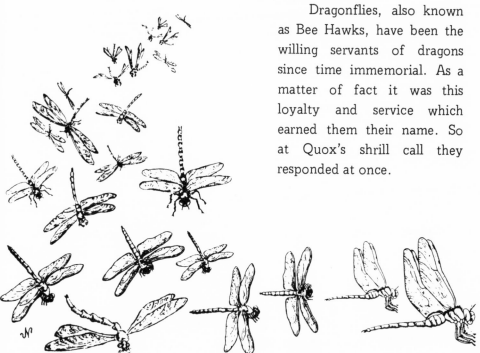

Dragonflies, also known as Bee Hawks, have been the willing servants of dragons since time immemorial. As a matter of fact it was this loyalty and service which earned them their name. So at Quox's shrill call they responded at once.

117

The Forbidden Garden

In a cloud of color they came, with their bodies of brown and bottle-green, metallic-blue and red, blazing with yellow stripes. Their black legs and net-like irridescent wings were almost twice as long as their bodies. The huge compound eyes of these swift, skillful fliers quickly located the bees. The sharp teeth and spined scoops, which lined their mouths were no longer retracted and masked. They were bared and ready to bite and tear. Although badly outnumbered by the bees, the dragonflies flung themselves upon their mortal enemies.

Oh, such a hum and buzz from the bumblebees as they fought to throw off their attackers. Oh, such a drone and whine from the dragonflies as they attempted to destroy the bumblebees. Back and forth across the garden raged the battle. Sometimes the bees had the advantage and sometimes the dragonflies. Then at a moment of crises, when the outcome of the battle seemed to swing in favor of the bees, a cloud of reinforcements arrived. The damosels had come.

The female dragonflies, with their shorter and more slender metallic-green and blue bodies, striped with yellow which gleamed like gold in the sunlight, were hardly less effective than their male counterparts. Their gossamer, amber colored wings drove them with even more speed and agility than the dragonflies —

and certainly with much more than the bees. Their presence turned the tide of battle and the bumblebees withdrew.

In the midst of all these noisy whirrings of wings, as each side stunted and maneuvered to gain position, Quox scrambled over the wall. He mounted his bicycle, and still clutching the now somewhat discordant bouquet, started for home. His departure, however, did not go completely unnoticed. One of the largest of the bumblebees, marking his attempted escape, eluded the dragonflies and set out in hot pursuit of Quox. He quickly overtook him, circled his head twice and stung Quox right on the end of his nose.

With a scream of anguish and pain Quox dropped his mother's bouquet and tumbled from his bicycle into the roadside ditch. His brand new bicycle, however, fell beneath one of the four massive, ironbound wheels of a heavily loaded wagon, which was passing. The crunch it made as it crushed the bicycle's front wheel called forth a new burst of anguish from Quox.

The driver of the wagon, furious because Quox had frightened his horses, got down from the wagon and gave Quox's smashed bicycle a kick.

"Why don't you look where you are going, you foolish dragon? You almost made me lose control of my wagon. Why can't you behave yourself and act as other dragons do?" exclaimed the carter.

And then, while Quox was trying to choke back his sobs, the man further stated, "I think that I will take this bicycle with me and keep it until I am certain that the front wheel of my cart is not damaged. And stop crying, you big sissy. What happened to your bike serves you right. You had no business here in the first place."

It was not fair of the carter to call Quox a sissy for despite his size he was quite young and tender, and he really was hurt. The terrible bee sting, right on the tip of his nose — which is a very tender spot on all dragons, plus the scrapes and bumps he had received when he fell off his bike, coupled with the damage to the front wheel of his new bicycle, was enough to make anyone cry.

And then the man added, "Been stealing flowers too, I'll be bound, or my name is not Carter."

This brought a response from Quox, at last, "You be quiet and leave me alone, you old farmer, and don't you dare touch my bike," he burst out, none too politely.

Then, pushing his broken bicycle in front of him, he started for home. Poor little dragonette, he was crying hot tears and thinking dire thoughts about what he would do to any carter he might meet when he grew up. The flowers of his mother's bouquet were crushed in his hot little paw, their tones muted and discordant.

This was a sorry spectacle that greeted his mother on his arrival at his home. And it was at this exact time that Tititi-Hoochoo delivered his verdict on Quox's conduct.

"Tubekins," said the Great Djinn, "thank you for bringing me word of Quox's latest escapade and thank you for your recommendation as to the punishment he should receive. However, I hardly need remind you of the honor bestowed on us when the dragon family was placed under our protection. Of the four lords of the animal kingdom: the Phoenix, the Unicorn, the Tortoise and the Dragon, I feel that the dragon reflects the highest qualities of strength, wisdom and vigilance. Dragons are not the terrifying, sinister creatures emblematic of evil, as depicted in fiction, rather they are friendly, benevolent and peaceful.

"Quox, despite contrary opinions held by some, is not the exception. One can hardly expect a baby of some six hundred and fifty summers to possess the gravity and self command of an adult. Quox's crime in picking the flowers was minimal. The law states a 'person' shall not pick the flowers and Quox is not a person. I grant you that this interpretation is merely a technicality and does not absolve Quox, but I believe that in this case justice has already been served. Quox has been sufficiently punished by the bumblebees and the wagon which damaged his bicycle. Therefore, no additional punishment will be inflicted.

"The incident will not be forgotten, however, and if Quox continues his disrespectful attitude toward his elders, which I consider most reprehensible, additional corrective action will be taken. Quox shall be informed of this verdict by his illustrious ancestor, the Original Dragon, Skanderbeg. I believe he will remember it."

Quox remembered it. He also never forgot the vivid remarks of his great, great, great grandparent, Skanderbeg, concerning his personality, clumsiness and lack of intelligence.

During this period of reflection, Quox had stared so long and piercingly at the carter that Mr. Wainwright had become very apprehensive and had begun to shuffle his feet in fear of the dragonel's next move.

Quox blinked and said gruffly, "I have been waiting for over two thousand years to repay a carter—any carter or wagoner—for an injury done me by a man named Carter when I was just a baby. Now the time has come that I may take my revenge." Quox paused and severely regarded the trembling man, then added, "Now that that time has come, I find that I have outgrown my childish desire for revenge. You may move your wagon."

With this statement Quox closed his eyes and seemed to sleep.

Chapter 10

The Mayor of Wagon Gap

ou may be sure," said the mayor, "that when the dragon gave his approval to move the wagon, Dcim Wainwright and his helpers lost no time in moving it to a safer place.

"Because I am the mayor of this town," he continued in his self satisfied manner, "the people pushed me forward toward the dragon. When I was almost to his chin, he opened his eyes and I caught a glint of red in them which was fearsome to behold. I admit that I was startled. A lesser man would have bolted, but instead I asked this monster who he was, where he came from and what he wanted.

"He spat out a piece of varied colored material. Here, I have it right here." The mayor pulled a piece of multi-colored gossamer from his pocket and showed it to Tip. "The dragon then told me that his name was Quox, and he described in detail the events which caused him to be here."

The mayor then related to Tip the story Quox had told him.

"It was almost unbelievable," the mayor went on, "and, of course, the dragon placed all the blame on some improbable sky fairy. The dragon further said that if we would give him a snack now and then he would not harm us, but that if he was not fed or if he was molested in any way he would knock down the rest of the village. He demonstrated his ability to do this by a sweep of his tail which completely demolished an ice cream and candy story standing at the end of the street.

"When I asked him what he wanted to eat, he replied that he was accustomed to snacking on three or four scuttles of live coals, every hour, and that he was hungry right then. He emphasized this by opening that tremendous mouth of his and running out his long red tongue.

"It took some doing, let me tell you, to get the charcoal burning just right and in the amounts he wanted, but we succeeded and have been feeding him for the past five hours or so. In between his snacks, as he calls them, he just lies there with his eyes either completely closed or slitted."

"What do you intend to do about this monster?" asked Tip.

"We have sent a messenger to our ruler in Emerald City, Princess Ozma, for help, but I am not altogether certain that even she can help us, for as you see it is such a big dragon. If Princess Ozma cannot help us then we can only petition Glinda, the Sorceress of OZ, and see what comes of that. After all we are loyal and trustworthy subjects and as such we need and expect help. If help is not forthcoming, and the dragon does not go away of his own accord, we will have no choice but to move away, leave our homes and businesses and start over again in some other place. This will not only be sad for us but will be a terrible misfortune to the OZ children who expect to receive the toys we make on their birthdays and other festivals."

"What type things do you make for children?" asked Tip.

"Before I answer that, let me welcome you, young man, and you too, whatever you are," he addressed the Sawhorse, "to Wagon Gap, Rosewood Meadows, the Land of the Quadlings. With a name like Wagon

Gap it would seem only logical for one to assume that we make wagons, which we do.

"Until this misfortune occurred," the Mayor went on, "we were a very thriving community and a very happy one. We made toy wagons, buggies, buckboards, shays, cabriolets and all other type conveyances for the children of OZ to play with. At times we even made full scale models, some of which you could have seen had not that dreadful dragon crushed them when he fell out of the sky. Those which he did not crush, when he fell on them, he smashed when he lashed his tail in rage when we approached him."

"Whatever gave you the notion to make these types of toys for the children?" asked Tip.

"Orginally we got our ideas on wagon-making from a book, which has been the property of the village for many, many years. We miniaturized the wagons and other conveyances, pictured in the book, and made them into toys and we even built some full-scale models for our own enjoyment. Our most important full-scale conveyence, which we have named the Red Wagon, thankfully suffered no damage. This wagon was designed and built by Mr. Wainwright, who got his idea from a poem about a one horse shay.* He calls it his masterpiece and claims that it will never wear out. Another important point about the Red Wagon is that it combines all the best features and styles of a wagonette, shay or carriage. In this way the vehicle will answer all her needs," he concluded.

"All whose needs?" asked Tip.

"Why Princess Ozma's of course. We have heard that she has no proper vehicle to ride in and that because of this she must ride on the back of a creature which apparently resembles that one of yours. This we think must be very uncomfortable as well as not very decorous for a princess. We were about to deliver the Red Wagon to her in Emerald City when this," he pointed at Quox, "arrived. However, when Princess Ozma comes here, in response to our plea to remove the dragon, we plan to pre-

* The Deacon's Masterpiece or The Wonderful "One-Hoss Shay"
  by Oliver Wendell Holmes

sent the wagon to her."

Tip, who had been listening to this discourse with only one ear, while studying the problem of the dragonel with the rest of his faculties, said to the mayor, "I have a plan to get rid of the dragonel, if you want to hear it."

A murmur ran through the group of men who had gathered around the mayor and Tip, and they exchanged glances as if to ask what a young boy, however brave, could do to solve their problem without causing the dragonel to do further damage to their village.

"We all recognize that you are a very brave young boy," one man said, "maybe so brave as to be foolhardy, and therein lies the problem. Foolhardiness may enrage the dragon so that he will thrash around and completely desolate the town. I for one do not think that we should pay any attention to your plan, but should continue to feed the dragon until either Princess Ozma or Glinda the Good comes. If we men have not been able to formulate a plan in the past five or six hours, I do not see how a child can come up with a workable plan on the spur of the moment. If the boy fails, the damage already done by the dragon will be nothing compared to what else he will do. That is what I think," he concluded, and there were murmurs of approval from many of the others who were gathered near.

"One moment!" said a woman who had been eyeing Tip for some time. "I think that we should hear what our mayor has to say on this subject. After all, we elected him because we had confidence in his ability to make decisions. And further, I for one would like to hear this youngster's idea for dealing with the dragon. I think there is more to 'him' than meets the eye."

Tip turned away from watching three of the men pour hods of hot coals into Quox's cavernous mouth, and as he caught the woman's eye she smiled at him, conspiratorially, and went inside her house.

The mayor raised his hand for quiet and said ponderously, "I agree with Evelita. I think we should hear the lad's plan and if we feel that it has merit, authorize him to carry it out. After all, we do not know how long it will take to get relief from the dragon from Princess Ozma or Glinda. So, go ahead, boy, tell us your plan."

While Tip was outlining his plan, others in OZ were wrestling with problems they felt to be of similar magnitude.

Chapter 11

Jellia Jamb

ne of Glinda's problems was how the presence of the dragonel on the road which Ozma was traveling would effect Ozma. Another was the problem about what to do with Jellia Jamb. If Ozma should meet with trouble would it not be better to have Jellia Jamb in Emerald City in the event Ozma should want to contact her. These were Glinda's problems and she pondered them for some time. Finally Glinda decided that it would be very cruel to leave Jellia Jamb in Emerald City alone with her worries, so Glinda acted. She called for the stork girls who drew her ivory and ruby chariot through the sky.

The remarkable thing about these girls was that, when not pulling Glinda's aerial chariot through the sky, they were just normal girls, but when they dressed in their transformation skins, they changed into graceful white storks, who pulled the sky chariot smoothly and rhythmically.

These maidens were the tallest and most sprightly misses in all

Rosewood Meadows, and were selected to be stork maidens because of their intelligence and trustworthiness as well as their strength and endurance. It was a great honor to be chosen for this group and the girls were fully aware of this honor.

"My dears," Glinda addressed them, "would you please put on your stork transforming skins and take my chariot to Emerald City. I would like to have Jellia Jamb, Princess Ozma's friend and confidant, brought here to me as soon as possible. Jellia will be waiting for you in Ozma's rose garden. And," she added to the leader of the girls, "tell her to notify the Scarecrow of what has occurred and direct him to remain in Ozma's palace, so that if Ozma needs to contact anyone there, he will be available."

She smiled her thanks to the stork girls as they filed out, and what is noteworthy is that not one of them, not even the leader, asked any questions about why they were being sent on this mission. They knew if Glinda wanted them to know, she would tell them. They were also aware of the fact that curiosity is seldom a virtue. In a short time they were winging their way toward Emerald City.

At the royal palace in Emerald City, Jellia Jamb struggled with her problem; that was to try to compose herself so that she would be able to help Ozma, if necessary. As she sat in one of the ivory and emerald satin occasional chairs in Ozma's suite, Jellia gathered her thoughts together, so she might explain the events of the morning to Glinda, calmly and coherently.

She remembered that at about 8:00 o'clock she went to Ozma's suite to awaken her. She was puzzled at this tardiness, for Ozma was usually an early riser who liked to walk in the garden and talk to her flowers before she ate her breakfast, usually served early in the morning. When she received no answer to her knocks or calls, she entered the room and found Ozma gone. A cursory search and some questions of the servants in the area was followed by a thorough search of the palace and the grounds. The only fact elicited, was from the Guardian of the South Gate who said

that the Sawhorse and a young boy, who was riding him, had sped out of Emerald City at the moment he had opened the gate — just a short while after sunrise.

This information did little to calm Jellia Jamb's fears about Ozma's well-being, for the Sawhorse was forever going off somewhere, without telling anyone. Jellia felt that her fears were well-founded, for it was not too long ago that Mombi and others had worked their evil on Ozma, and she, Jellia Jamb, was constantly worried lest another kidnapping, or worse, should occur.

Jellia Jamb is a short, chubby, young Gillikin girl with hazel eyes and a mischievous sense of humor. She is the daughter of Jimb Jamb, a neighbor of Tip and Mombi in the Land of Purple Mountains. While back in the Gillikin country Jellia had made several attempts to get to know Tip better, but Mombi had always intervened and turned aside her overtures. So she had never really gotten acquainted with Tip. She had always detested Mombi, for Jellia was a friendly and outgoing girl — just opposite of the nasty old Mombi.

Jellia was adventurous and enterprizing and thus was dissatisfied with the calm and quiet Gillikin farm life. She yearned for the gaiety and excitement of city life and dreamed of the time she would be there. The locus of her dreams was Emerald City, for it was not only the capital of OZ but was, to all intents and purposes, the only really, truly city in OZ. So she teased and hectored her father until he intervened for her with the Good Witch of the North. This kind lady was able to get Jellia Jamb a position as maid in the royal palace, which the Wizard of Oz was just completing.

Prior to her departure she had several talks with the good witch, who explained to her many of the intricacies of palace life and instructed her in the customs and mores found in Emerald City. The day before she departed, the Good Witch told her of the disappearance of Ozma and bade her to be ever alert as to the whereabouts of the baby. Further, she told Jellia that any information she might come by relating to any suspicious actions on anyone's part should be reported to Glinda the Good, immediately. So off went Jellia, full of dreams and anticipations.

Upon her arrival at the palace, she was outfitted in a dainty green silk skirt which reached to her knees and was flared out by nine petticoats, eight of which were green, honoring Emerald City, and one was purple, honoring the Land of Purple Mountains, the region from which she had come. It is a custom in all royal households for the maids to wear nine petticoats.

She also wore green silk stockings embroidered with pea pods, and green satin slippers with tiny heads of lettuce for decoration instead of buckles and bows. Upon her silken blouse, clover leaves were appliqued, and she wore a jaunty little jacket trimmed with sparkling emeralds.

Her sweet disposition and willingness to work, even to do more than her share, was soon noted and made her a prime favorite with all. During this time at the palace she had known the Wizard, Dorothy Gale and Toto, the Scarecrow, Tin Woodman and the Cowardly Lion. Later, when the Scarecrow ruled OZ, he made Jellia Jamb the Housekeeper of the Royal Palace, and during that time she had become acquainted with Jack Pumpkinhead, the Sawhorse, H.M. Woggle-Bug T.E. and the Gump. She had also watched Tip with affection when he was in Emerald City after he had run away from Mombi. She had not mentioned their earlier acquaintanceship to him and he had not recognized her.

Then, after Ozma had been returned to her rightful body, Jellia Jamb became Ozma's personal maid, confidant and even teacher during Ozma's difficult transition from a boy to a girl. Jellia Jamb was merry, quick-witted, and vivacious, always fun loving and in high spirits — unless there was cause to worry about Ozma. She adored Ozma and Ozma fully returned her love.

Too upset to remain seated quietly for any length of time, Jellia left Ozma's boudoir and made her way down the broad staircase, through the long halls and out onto the park-like formal gardens. She walked slowly and quietly on the gravelled walks so deep in thought that she hardly noticed the beds of gorgeous flowers bordering the walks, or heard the lively song of birds and the drone of insects. She neared the green granite walls, which served primarily as a backdrop for the shrubs and flowers, riotous with color, and sat down on a cream colored bench.

She remembered another lovely day when Ozma, she and another girl had come to this very park to play. It was not so long ago either, and Ozma had been a girl again for only a few days. Down they came, three happy youngsters, singing as they skipped along the marble walks to the gravel path, where they broke into a run. Ozma had yet to learn that her hips and thighs worked differently, now that she was a girl, and that her torso did not seem to unlock as it had in the past, so running awkwardly, she stumbled and fell. But, assisted by pullings and tuggings and encouraged by sympathetic clucks, she got to her feet and went on a little less hastily.

The sun was hot on the soft green grass and the girls were skylarking and frisking like fawns, when Ozma noticed a football lying on the grass. She picked it up, fondled it as an old friend then tossed it into the air several times. While she played with the ball she noticed how small and delicate her hands had become, and she wondered if she could still pass the football as she had done in the past. So she called out to Jellia to catch the ball, faded back a few steps, cocked her arm and threw. The result was disaster; the ball fell almost to her feet and Ozma crumpled down in a heap, biting her lip to keep back the tears. It was not the hands which had worked the treachery, it was the shoulder. Her shoulder felt as if it had been pulled from its socket. It was then that Ozma realized that she could no longer throw things as she had when she was a boy.

There were many other things that she could no longer do, and, Jellia thought ruefully, many new things that she must learn to do. But Jellia was a patient teacher and Ozma an apt pupil, excepting of course the few times when she absolutely refused to do those 'sissy things.' Eventually though, she did them, and under Jellia's gentle but perserving tutelage these rebellions became fewer and fewer, and Ozma learned and practiced the graces inherent in her nature.

Jellia smiled to herself at these recollections and began walking with a more lively step toward the rose garden. In this large, sunken garden were masses of rose trees, kaleidoscopic in color and almost overwhelming in perfume. This was Ozma's favorite place, and is the most beautiful garden in OZ — or anywhere else for that matter.

Jellia Jamb

While Jellia waited for Glinda's chariot she was joined by the Scarecrow, and before she had time to become impatient, the amazing ivory chariot, drawn by the nine snow-white stork maidens, came into view over the city wall. It slowly circled the rose garden, then landed noiselessly in the center of the garden. After speaking with the leader of the stork maidens Jellia gave the Scarecrow Glinda's message, and in a trice the chariot was airborne.

She could not resist, indeed no one flying over Emerald City could ever resist, looking down at its magnificence. The view of the royal palace was breathtaking. Long green pennants streamed from the many towers, which were so very tall and stately they seemed to pierce the heavens. The massive light green granite wall, which embraced the city was crenelated and pierced from place to place with embrasures. The mighty gates, studded with huge emeralds, and framed with green veined white marble, stood ajar.

The entire Emerald City seemed to be a place of comfortable, old-fashioned solidity, with gates that welcomed rather than repelled. This feeling of peace and hominess was accentuated by the blaze of color from the flowers, cultivated in the embrasures of the wall and in the steps of the crenelations. Ivy covered the walls, adjacent to the gates.

There were countless small parks and squares, circuses and malls, as well as many small shops and businesses inside the wall. Many places, such as tea houses and candy shops, were actually combined with the home of the owner. These buildings generally had two stories. The many private homes in the city reflected their owner's varied tastes in architecture and construction materials, but all retained the unique OZ feature — two tall chimneys. The houses were crowded together in the city, but outside the walls they were located much farther apart. Even those outside the wall were considered part of the city.

The strong wings of the lovely stork maidens carried the chariot and its passenger effortlessly through the sky. Houses below, became more widely dispersed. Then suddenly the predominately green color of the landscape changed and became red as the chariot passed over the Quad River. In a short time it passed over the Hill of the Hammerheads, and a few moments later landed at Glinda's red marble palace.

Jellia Jamb immediately jumped to the ground, where she was met by a prettily uniformed girl soldier who took Jellia directly to Glinda's study, where Jellia expostulated,

"Oh, Glinda, where is she? Is she all right? What has happened?"

"Calm yourself child," soothed Glinda, "and be welcome. Ozma is all right. I have been told by my thrush that Ozma and the Sawhorse have their heads together. Ozma seems to be planning something."

Chapter 12

Tip Overcomes The Dragonel

s Tip prepared to put his plan into action, the mayor began to try to clear the street, and by way of explanation said,

"Folks, let's all go back inside and give the lad and his Sawhorse a chance to rid our town of this terrible dragon. The boy has described his plan to me and I have approved it."

"Then tell us what the plan is, Mayor," demanded one of the men as the crowd began to move away toward the shelter of the buildings.

"No, I do not think it advisable to discuss his plan out here where the dragon might overhear the details. Further, as your mayor, I already have given my approval to the plan and really see no reason why it should be discussed any more. You will all see the results in a very few moments."

This remark was greeted by some grumbling from the citizens, so the mayor added, "Very well, let's all go inside and there I will explain to you the details of our plan.''

With this statement, he moved off rapidly to the protection of one of the houses, and his action was followed by the crowd, many of whom squeezed into the same house as the mayor, while others sought refuge in nearby buildings.

The last census of OZ had numbered the population of Wagon Gap at 258 persons. This figure included many who lived on farms in the vicinity and were not present in the village at this time. There were probably not more than sixty or seventy people, including children, gathered in the street to watch the dragonel. For not even all the people of the village by any means had exchanged the security of their homes for the hazard of the street.

Tip in the meantime had bent down and was whispering instructions into the Sawhorse's ear. That worthy listened attentively and nodded his head several times in apparent agreement. Tip then moved back with the crowd until he was out of sight of the dragonel. He then worked his way slowly and cautiously through the yards and porches of the buildings which lined the street until he was standing near Quox's left shoulder, He was, however, out of direct view of the dragonel. There he stood and waited until the Sawhorse carried out his part of the project.

Quox, who had had his eyes closed while chewing his basket of red-hot coals, had not noticed Tip's approach. But, as soon as there were no more coals to be chewed Quox slowly opened his eyes and did notice something else which caused a sudden thin and piercing streak of red to gleam out from under the drooping lid of his right eye. The Sawhorse had approached and was staring at him with unconcealed malevolence. Quox at once raised up on all four legs, opened his long, fearful retractible claws, drew in a long breath and prepared to expel enough flames to incinerate the Sawhorse completely.

But the Sawhorse spoke, "Dragon, I will ask you a riddle and if you can solve it, I will not bother you further. If you cannot solve it, you will be bothered further. But, even if you lose no harm will come to you. You have a hundred seconds to answer the riddle once I have asked it. Agreed?"

Quox slowly let out his breath, and still keeping a wary eye on the Sawhorse turned this proposition over in his mind several times. Then, certain that any dragon could solve any riddle propounded by any ignorant sawhorse, he snorted his agreement.

The riddle game is sacred and of immense antiquity, and no dragon, however young and tender, can resist its fascination. It is so sacred that even wicked creatures are afraid to cheat when playing it. Ozma knew this and knew the dragon knew it.

Here is the riddle asked by the Sawhorse:

'A box without hinges, key or lid,
'Yet golden treasure inside is hid.'

Quox closed his eyes and thought and then he thought some more. He pondered and mused, deliberated and considered, reflected, examined and appraised. It was all to no avail. He grew angry and hissed and sputtered to himself. He puffed and fumed and his breath, which at first had smelled of salt and pepper, began to develop a decided stench of brimstone. The sky-blue scales on his head began to glow and took on a scarlet hue, and his tail twitched spasmodically. He clenched his eyes shut tightly, and made no reply.

Then the Sawhorse exclaimed triumphantly, "You lose dragon. You have had your allotted time. You lose!"

As soon as the Sawhorse had said to Quox that his time to solve the riddle was up and that he had lost — but while the dragonel's eyes were still tightly closed — Tip did one of the bravest things he had ever done. He ran under the dragonel's massive shoulder and, crouching down, scurried up to Quox's chin.

Even though Tip did not touch the dragonel, Quox sensed his presence. His enormous body stiffened and his fire belched forth from his mouth, His hideous shriek of wrath and fear was deafening and his hot breath shrivelled the plants about him. When under the dragonel's chin, Tip stood erect and with his hands clutched together began to rub frantically at the underside of Quox's heavily scaled chin.

Tip knew that if he could get close enough to a dragon, without being bitten, eaten or incinerated by its breath, and could stroke the reptile under the chin he could put it to sleep. He did not know, however, how long he would have to rub Quox's chin before Quox would fall asleep. So he continued this stroking for what seemed to him an age, but in reality was only a few short moments.

Then, just as his wearied arms and blistered hands began to fail, the dragonel shuddered and gave a convulsive spasm. The huge body, with its proportionately huge head began to collapse onto the ground as Quox fell asleep. Tip, still struggling to stroke the underside of Quox's jaw, felt the dragonel's weight begin to settle on him and crush him. He scrambled on hands and knees and finally crawled out from under Quox's ponderous body. He emerged to the shouts and cries of encouragement from the Quadlings, many of whom had come back out onto the street.

Quox was now fully asleep, with only wisps of smoke coming from his nostrils—because his fires were always low in slumber. But Tip did not know how long the dragonel would stay asleep. So, without delay, he took the ribbon of the eighth color, which he had brought with him from Emerald City, out of his pocket, clambered up the monstrous jaw, over one immense eye and placed the ribbon securely on the dragonel's neck. Then to the gasps of astonishment from the assembled Quadlings, the body of the dragonel began to shrink, and in about as much time as it takes to tell, Quox was reduced in size to a creature about a foot long, including his tail. He continued to sleep as Tip picked him up, tied the ribbon in a bow and gently carried him back to where the Quadlings were congregated.

Tip Overcomes The Dragonel

None of this activity had escaped the notice of two red-breasted thrushes who were perched in a tall tree. They surveyed the situation, peered closely at Tip, and chattered together for a moment. One then flew off to the south.

Then as the villlagers realized that the dragon was small and helpless and no longer was a menace to them, they became unruly. All that were not already in the street poured out from the buildings and began to cry for vengeance against the dragon.

"Destroy the dragon!" cried some. "Tear off his legs and cut off his head," screamed others, and yet others screamed, "Punish him for what he did to our village. Give him to us, boy, and we will take care of him."

"No!" exclaimed Tip. "Wisdom overcame him, not force and violence, so force and violence will not now be used. I promised him that he would not be harmed and I will not allow any harm to come to him. How can you expect him to learn the virtues of kindness and gentleness when you now plan to treat him with hate and brutality? Leave him to me and I will see that he does not do any more harm."

At this moment the mayor pushed forward and cried out, "Leave the lad alone. He has done what he said he would do. He has saved the town. He has overcome the dragon in his own way, and I say let him carry out the rest of his plan in his own way. We owe him a debt of gratitude, not a roughing up."

But in spite of these pleas, a tall burly man with spiky red-hair bulled his way past the mayor. He raised both arms for silence and shouted,

"Hear me, fellow citizens, I know all about dragons. I know that they are either worms or lizards, and each is as bad as the other. They are sly, cruel, evil monsters. They destroy for the pure joy of destruction and they will steal anything and everything they lay eyes on. Then they take that treasure which they steal and secrete it in subterranean dragon hoards away from the light of day and the eyes of man. Never trust dragons or those who attempt to protect them. Dragons are fated to be destroyed and have been destroyed by men for countless ages. Let us not change our habits now. Destroy the dragon!"

Although this man did not know anything at all about dragons, his remarks further inflamed the people. They began to press forward and might have actually destroyed Quox had not the red-haired man pushed Tip to the ground as he tried to wrestle the little dragonel from him. Because Tip was holding the tiny sleeping creature to his breast to protect him, Tip fell so hard that his cap flew off, unloosing a cloud of long thick hair, the fineness and color of pallid gold. The man stopped! The people gasped! The Sawhorse acted!

"Stop, you fools, and recognize your ruler. This is Princess Ozma of OZ." So spake the Sawhorse. A flash of lightning accompanied his words, and the rain came.

Chapter 13

The Cloud Fairies

he day which had dawned so beautifully had changed. Overhead a bank of dark, low nimbus clouds, thick as unspun cotton, had loomed up so suddenly and was scudding across the sky so rapidly that some might think its presence was caused by magic. And they would be right. Those fat, sullen looking clouds, now dumping their cargoes of rain, had come at Ozma's behest. She had solicited the Rainbow King's aid and he, in his home in the clouds, had granted her request.

The bewildering homes of the sky fairies, including that of the Rainbow King, are very hard to describe. They are bewildering because they are not at all like the houses we are accustomed to. The sky fairies' houses are the clouds, and the clouds are ever changing, so the house one fairy has today will not be either the same house or even in the same place tomorrow.

The clouds which form these homes are known as cirrus because they are lofty clouds, seemingly loose and feathery in appearance, although substantial enough to house the sky fairies very comfortably. These are the highest clouds in the sky so it is almost impossible to make out the details of these temporary residences from the ground. They are also ever changing because of the wind and the activity of the Yagmurs.

Yagmurs are creatures who are normally about the size of house cats. They have no tails but have exceedingly long proboscises, which they insert into the clouds and draw the moisture from them. The Yagmurs are absolutely colorless, that is to say, transparent or invisible except for their eyes — which are large as plums and purple as grapes. The moisture in clouds is the Yagmur's only sustenance and, as they are exceedingly hungry by nature, their voracious appetites often get them into trouble.

At times they enter the cloudlet homes of sky fairies, and before the occupants realize what is happening a Yagmur will have completely reduced their home to nothingness by sucking all the moisture out of the cloud walls, floors and ceilings. The sky fairies, justifiably indignant over this outrage, sometimes give chase to the Yagmurs, but to no avail for the only thing they can see to chase are two purple eyes and a misty body of water.

The Yagmur, who after absorbing an entire house has grown to tremendous proportions, attempts to escape. He does this by expelling through his proboscis the water he has taken in. This acts as a jet and he is propelled far away at a tremendous speed. As he expels the water it sometimes douses his pursuers, which does not improve either their temper or their love for this odd creature.

If the chase continues too long the Yagmur loses all the water he has ingested for nourishment and which has given him his great size, so he again becomes just a small, frightened, hungry little entity — so shy and pitiful that no one would have the heart to punish him.

The extremely kind hearted and gentle daughters of the rainbow are trusted by the Yagmurs, who in time of peril seek refuge with them, and even at other times join with the fairies in their practical jokes. If someone, anyone for that matter, should be lounging sleepily, in a cloud chair when the rainbow fairies think he should be up and about, the rainbow

The Cloud Fairies

fairies would surely bring in one of the Yagmurs and stick his proboscis into the chair. He would, of course, gratefully suck out all the moisture and dump the chair's occupant onto the floor—amid gales of laughter from the fairies. This, of course, is only one of the many tricks the Yagmurs can be trained to perform.

There are also cloudlet fights, similar to pillow fights and snowball throws in other climes, where the girls choose up sides and throw small rainballs at each other. Each fairy arms herself with a supply of rainballs and a Yagmur for a shield. As the Yagmurs are exceedingly quick and agile, they are able to catch many of the rainballs and suck them dry before they reach their targets. Sometimes they miss, but after all that is the fun of the game. Then, when the battle is over and the girls retire to dry off and change, the Yagmurs swallow up the mess left by the leaky rainballs.

It has been noted by some of the rare visitors to these areas that many of these beautiful cloud houses have tall, candy-striped pillars which support a roof of light clouds. These pillars stand on much more substantial floors of congealed clouds and thus are more permanent than those houses without pillars. Cloud sofas and lounges abound and the beds are made of the softest and fleeciest cloudlets.

Sky fairies, particularly the daughters of the rainbow, usually go to bed quite early in the evening so lighting presents no great problem. But if for one reason or another it is necessary for them to stay up at night, light is furnished by a large prism. This prism captures and stores light from the sun during the day and sends these rays forth at night. The strange colorations sometimes seen in cirrus clouds are caused by these prismatic rays.

Sky fairies are little concerned with food, and therefore, eat very little. Their diet consists mainly of dewdrops and a few tiny beaten biscuits. They have been known at times, particularly when on earth to eat ice cream and perhaps even a small piece of chicken—white meat only, of course.

The Cloud Fairies

There are other clouds, besides the ones they live in, which afford the sky fairies playgrounds, dancing pavilions and soft cushions to laze on and dream. These clouds take many shapes; sometimes thick and heavy, sometimes sheer and fleecy, and sometimes thin and scattered. And if a person lies on his back and watches these clouds drift by, he will see many different formations appear and disappear.

Sometimes, dense, cottony cumulus clouds appear to resemble great galleons, under full sail, cruising majestically across the sky. A close look might reveal Polychrome and her sisters acting as captain and crew of this great cloud ship. The girls appear as little flashes of color as they reef some sails, furl others, and even at times change the entire contour of the ship. These mischievious girls play such pranks that the galleon may be changed into an entirely different object.

Other times they like to push and pull at the smaller rounded masses of clouds, building castles of them and then marching back and forth on the battlements and ramparts as little soldiers. Then they sculp from the clouds other strange faces and graceful and beautiful designs.

They dearly love to dance and particularly so on days when the winds aloft push the clouds so hard that they break into long streaks and present a 'mackerel sky' appearance. Then a sharp eye might detect the sky fairies swirling and pirouetting from one flat 'bony looking' cloud to another.

Dancing! That is the first love of all these enchanting creatures of the sky. They dance on rainbows, through and over clouds, and in their own fragile homes, and they are so sure-footed that they seldom, if ever, fall from a cloud or slip off the rainbow. This does happen, occasionally, and even though the girls are uncomfortable for a little while, there is no real harm done and the girls soon rejoin their sisters. Singing, dancing and laughing, that is how they spend their time. So it is of little wonder that the sky fairies are the happiest and most contented of all beings.

And of these, surely the happiest and most contented are the daughters of the rainbow. Actually they are the daughters of the Rainbow King, who is the brother of the great Rain King. These girls have the pleasant and enviable task of giving color to the rainbow when it appears. After each rain the Rainbow King causes a transparent arc, which is the actual rainbow, to curve down to the ground. Then his daughters, clad in their many colored robes, dance down the rainbow to the point where it touches the ground.

The robes or draperies, which the daughters of the rainbow wear consist of innumerable pleats running the full length of the robe. Each pleat is irridescent on one side and of the eighth color on the other. As the girls dance, the light from the sun catches the irridescent panels of the pleat and reflects all the colors of the spectrum. As the robe moves and the other panel is exposed to the sun, it reflects a softness which mutes the glare of the irridescence and makes the color from each panel meld into the other and cause a running flow of rainbow colors.

The rainbow does not usually remain in place for a long time; it generally stays just long enough for the fairies to dance down to the ground and then dance up to the clouds again. Of all the sisters, Polychrome was the most daring, and while she had never fallen or slipped, she had at times scampered off the rainbow and touched the ground. She would quickly rejoin her sisters because the ground felt cold to her feet and gave her goose-bumps.

The bank of rain clouds over Wagon Gap moved on its way across the Deadly Desert and the rain which had fallen for only a twinkling stopped as suddenly as it had started. The rainbow commenced its descent and with it came the rainbow daughters, led by Polychrome.

This time, however, Polychrome did not scamper happily off the rainbow. She stepped off quietly, knowing that she had been summoned, knowing why she had been summoned, and knowing that she must obey that summons.

Chapter 14

Quox Goes Home

complete hush fell over the assemblage and movement halted as a beautiful rainbow touched the ground in the middle of Wagon Gap's main street. Ozma rose slowly, still holding the dragonel, walked to the edge of the rainbow and waited for Polychrome to approach her.

Awe maintained silence as the villagers saw these two fairy princesses meet. Polychrome was beautiful almost beyond compare. Her face was colored tenderly and softly. Her eyebrows arched high above her long lashed grey eyes. Her nose was delicate and saucy and her chin impudence incarnate. She was dressed in almost transparent gossamer, spangled with dewdrops and edged with silver gauze. But she cast down her eyes at the beauty of Ozma, which she could see even through the smoke and grime that covered Ozma's face and the wet ungainly clothes which covered her body.

As always, Ozma was gracious and, while smiling a welcome to Polychrome, said, "You are indeed the most beautiful fairy I have ever seen.

Welcome to OZ."

"Thank you Your Majesty," replied Polychrome, who was charmed by this compliment and hung out the sign of it on her cheeks. "It is indeed a pleasure to meet you and I wish that I could stay with you longer, but you must excuse me please, for the rainbow will soon be lifting and I must not be left behind. My father said that he would punish me severely if I failed to climb on the bow this time when he lifted it."

"My dear," said Ozma, "I have an urgent matter to discuss with you, and the rainbow will remain here until I have finished."

So the Quadlings were treated to the sight of a dazzling, pulsating rainbow remaining in place while Ozma explained her desires to Polychrome. She told of Quox's misadventures after his arrival in OZ, of her actions and of the actions of the Sawhorse, including the riddle.

"As most of this affair resulted from you teasing Quox," Ozma reminded Polychrome, "it is only proper that you return him to the Great Djinn's realm. The rainstorm we just had is moving off to the west, and very soon will shower on the Land of Ev, under which lies the domain of the Nomes, whose ruler is Roquat the Red. I want you to take Quox onto the rainbow and keep him with you until the bow descends close by the entrance to the Black Hole.

"No, no, it will not take long, only a few minutes, for the entrance is located quite near to one of the passages to the Nome King's regions. So be careful; you know what Roquat the Red has done to the royal family of Ev. Then as soon as the rainbow touches ground, carry Quox to the Black Hole, take the ribbon from his neck and drop him into the tube."

"I'm not afraid of the Nome King for I am a sky fairy and he can do nothing to harm me, but I am a little frightened of Quox. Does he bite?" asked Polychrome.

"No, he's a nice dragonel for a dragon," replied Ozma, "and besides, he will remain asleep and tiny until he arrives at his sublunar home. The The ribbon you see around his neck has not only erased everything from

Quox Goes Home

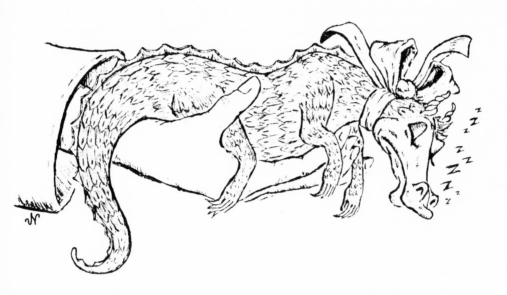

his memory from the time he fell into the tube, but will also keep him asleep until it is removed. Now take him and dance up your rainbow.

"Oh, one last thing Polychrome, if news of this escapade of Quox were ever to be known publicly it would greatly embarrass Tititi-Hoochoo, therefore, please never mention anything about what has taken place here today to anyone."

"I promise that I will never mention this to anyone under any circumstances, not only because it was foolish of me to tease Quox, but also because I certainly do not want to distress the Great Djinn. Tell me, Ozma, how did you know that this dragon is Quox and that he fell into the Black Hole chasing me? Did Tititi-Hoochoo tell you?

"No," replied Ozma, "Quox told his story to the mayor of this town, and the mayor told me. As you know, a dragon cannot lie; he can dissemble, conceal the truth or put an untrue appearance on it, but he cannot lie. If a dragon is asked a direct question he must either answer truthfully or remain silent. Quox, when asked a direct question by the mayor, answered it truthfully and although the mayor did not know it, I knew that Quox was telling the truth. And I assure you Sky Fairy, that I knew the mayor was telling the truth for no one, no one at all, can lie to me."

As the two girls kissed goodbye, Polychrome whispered to Ozma," I will never rest until you tell me the answer to the riddle that the Saw-horse put to Quox. I am not very good at riddles," she confessed.

"An egg," answered Ozma with a smile, then watched Polychrome, holding Quox somewhat gingerly, twirl and spin into her sisters' arms, where they all dissolved into a swirl of color as the rainbow lifted and faded into the distance.

The villagers, during this conversation, began to nudge each other and ask each other what was being said, for even though they could hear the conversation they could not understand it. This was because Ozma and Polychrome were communicating in Fairie, which is distinct from any other language and understood only by very few fairies. It is also well to remember that when speaking this language, if one desires to direct his remarks to one other particular person, no other person, no matter how close to the speaker he is standing, can comprehend what is being said. Of course no one would be so ill-mannered as to try to eaves-drop another's private conversation, so this stricture is proof against one accidently overhearing another's words.

As for the language of OZ itself, it is not necessary for one to go to school to learn to speak or understand it. Speech is merely the oral repre-sentation of thoughts, and thoughts are universally the same no matter what language is being spoken at the time. As these thought impulses are stronger in so-called fairylands than in other places, strangers or new-comers to OZ have no trouble either talking to or understanding the Ozians. Visitors, unless informed to the contrary, actually believe that the Ozians are speaking the visitor's language.

Quox Goes Home

In the Great Djinn's realm the Peculiar Person was pruning roses when an object shot out of the Black Hole and fell almost at his jet-black feet. Surprised, he stopped his work, walked over to it and picked it up. It was a very tiny dragonel, not a dragon nor a dragonette.

"I wonder where this creature came from and why it is wearing this strange ribbon around its neck," puzzled Tubekins.

Now this was Quox for certain and still asleep and small, because Polychrome had been disobedient. Being a girl, she was squeamish about handling reptiles and even though she was a sky fairy she was afraid of Quox. So she had not removed the ribbon, as Ozma had asked her to do, before she dropped Quox into the Black Hole.

Still, puzzled, Tubekins picked up the sleeping, miniature dragonel, held it close to his scarlet robe, and removed the ribbon.

"Get off me you great big lout!" screamed Tubekins, who had suddenly recognized Quox. "You are crushing me and all the roses in the garden. Must you always demolish everything, everytime, everywhere you are?"

"It's not my fault," whined Quox, who had awakened and regained his great size as soon as the ribbon had been removed. "I don't remember anything. Not even how I got here. All I know is that the toe of my left foot hurts infernally and that I have growing pains in my wings."

"Your wings? You are not old enough by 500 years to have wings. Those are just buds," retorted Tubekins, spitefully.

"Now get out of my garden and await the call from the Great Djinn for I am going right now and tell him about this. He will take care of you. Now get out of here."

Quox, abashed, departed.

Chapter 15

The Red Wagon

ith the departure of Quox and Polychrome, the mayor bustled up to Ozma's side, called out to the townspeople and began to make a speech. His effort, however, was short lived for one of the women—the one who had been eyeing Tip narrowly even before he was recognized as Ozma—interrupted.

"Mr. Mayor, why don't you talk with Mr. Wainwright about the Red Wagon? This is no time for speeches. Princess Ozma has apparently travelled a long way to help us and is exhausted, scorched and scratched, also, she is undoubtedly hungry. So save your speeches while I take this child to my home for a wash, a rest and a bite to eat. She may be a princess and a ruler of OZ to some, but to me she is also a tired begrimed little girl.

"It is not necessary for you to accompany us," she said to the mayor, who had begun to walk with them, "I know the way to my own home by this time." With that remark she put her arm around Ozma and

The Red Wagon

they walked together to her house.

Like almost every house in OZ, this one was circular, with a domed roof and two tall chimneys. Inside was a living room, kitchen and dining area, two bedrooms and a bath, plus an attic. All the rooms had high ceilings and there were no square corners where the walls met.

"This is one of the smaller houses," the woman said as she led Ozma to one of the bedrooms, "but it is just perfect for my husband and me. It is small enough to keep clean, without too much effort, and yet large enough to be comfortable. There are towels and things in the bathroom. Help yourself and take your time. If you want rest, lie down on that bed."

After a quick wash and brush-up, Ozma, although still very tired and stiff, came out through the bedroom — where the bed looked very inviting indeed — and went into the cool darkness of the living room. The shades were drawn, and lamps, dependent from wall sconces, gave off only a faint glow. This was a cozy room with a hardwood floor, covered with throw rugs, and furnished with upholstered chairs and a sofa. Drawn up in front of the dark wood and brick fireplace were two comfortable looking wooden rocking chairs.

The Red Wagon

"I am here in the kitchen, Princess," called out the woman. "Would you like to come in here or shall I serve you in the living room?"

"The kitchen, by all means," answered Ozma, and then asked, "Won't you please tell me your name?"

"My name is Evelita Bayan. Please call me Evelita."

"With pleasure, Evelita," replied Ozma as she walked through the archway into the kitchen and dining area.

Here in this bright and cheery room, with its gay chintz curtains, were butcher blocks and counters and many cupboards — jealously guarding their contents. Fresh made cheeses and garlands of dried fruit and vegetables hung from the rafters. Dominating all, was the huge stone and brick fireplace, with a spit in place and a kettle bubbling merrily away. The exotic aroma of spices, which crept out from the larder, tugged at Ozma's nostrils and brought visions of goodies to her mind.

The two chimneys and fireplaces, which are unique in OZ houses, serve very useful purposes. The power used to warm and light the house, cook the food, and heat the water is furnished by ultraviolet rays, which come from the sun on all days — either cloudy or clear. The sliding doors between the rooms open and close on command and are also powered by these rays.

"This source of power is wonderful," Evelita said to Ozma. "Those chimneys act as positive and negative poles, I am told. I really do not understand the principle of this power source, but my husband says he does."

"We are also able to use our fireplaces for cooking and just for comfort," explained Evelita. "While I appreciate solar power, I also like a cheery fire on a cold evening, and as for cooking, there are some things which taste better when cooked over an open fire," continued Evelita, who did not know that Ozma had once lived in a similar house in the Land of Purple Mountains.

"Now, if you are ready, we will have a little lunch " invited the Quadling lady, and they both sat down to a glass-topped bamboo table loaded with food. There were triangular red loaves of freshly baked bread,

159

sprinkled with sesame seeds and served with masses of butter, honey and clotted cream, sweet, juicy melons, barley fried with cheese — soft and doughy and so delicious — and there were nuts, fat sweet berries and seed cakes to top it all off.

Just as they were finishing their luncheon, Ozma noticed many little noses pressed against the panes of the kitchen and dining room windows. The noses belonged to the children of Wagon Gap who were curious to get a better look at the lovely girl who was their ruler. This is not to say that the adults were not also curious, but the inhibitions which maturity brings many times precludes grown-ups from showing their natural feelings.

"Princess," Evelita said, "if I thought the house was not entirely surrounded by my fellow townsmen, I would try to spirit you away via the back door for I know how tired you are. But I am afraid that the beseigers have cut off all avenues of escape. And I must tell you that the villagers have arranged a ceremony and presentation for you and it would disappoint them terribly if you did not attend. So if you are finished we will go out into the city square where the mayor, after the fashion of all politicians, wants to take this occasion to make a speech. I firmly believe that he has to make a speech every so often, or he will become so full of words that he will swell up and explode. And we do not want that to happen, do we?"

So Ozma was led, smiling and waving, out of the house, down the street, which was thronged with cheering people — many waving small OZ flags — to a place of honor on the front steps of the imposing meeting house. There she stood beside the mayor, listening to the cheers and shouts of the crowd as they noisily showed their love and esteem for her. This was the first time, excepting times in Emerald City, that Ozma had met with her subjects as their Queen, and their manifestations of regard and affection touched her deeply and brought tears of gratitude to mingle with her smile of happiness.

The mayor, anxious to get on with his speech, was waving his arms and calling for quiet, and when the crowd's exuberance had subsided somewhat, he began:

"Your Majesty, friends . . . , I mean, Your Majesty, I would like . . . I mean, we would like, that is to say, the citizens of Wagon Gap and I would like to thank you again, formally, for ridding our fair village of that dreadful dragon. If a man had done what you did, it would be considered a magnificent achievement. If a boy had done it, it would be considered miraculous, but for a young girl to have done it—well, words fail to describe the true dimensions of the exploit. We are indeed honored . . ." he continued. And he continued and continued, while the minutes grew in number and his audience grew restless.

Finally, he stated, "And in conclusion . . ." and went on to restate all that he had previously said. He then sat down.

Ozma, fortunately, had been provided a comfortable chair so had not been forced to stand and listen to this interminable harangue.

The Red Wagon

As the mayor sat down, benign and smiling in self-satisfaction at his fine flow of words, his wife poked him in the ribs and hissed a few words into his ear.

Back on his feet as if stung by a hornet, he exclaimed, "Oh yes, Your Majesty, may I present one of our finest workmen, a man who has made for you a token of our respect and devotion. Mr. Wainwright. Mr. Wainwright was an apprentice to Mr. Smith of Smith and Tinker, Ev,* until his unfortunate accident—Mr. Smith's accident I mean. A little after that accident Mr. Wainwright immigrated to OZ and brought with him the vast store of knowledge he had gained during his period of apprenticeship with Smith and Tinker."

As the mayor took a breath preparatory to continuing his harangue, for all politicians—particularly mayors—love to hear the sound of their own voices, a man stood up beside him and interrupted.

"Thank you for your introduction, Mr. Mayor. Your Majesty, my name is Dcim Wainwright and I am honored to have the privilege of meeting you. I will not detain you for long for I am certain that you want to continue your journey as soon as possible. So I will just say that I am here to present you, on behalf of the entire village, with the Red Wagon, and tell you a little of how it came to be made.

"This enchanted wagon is unique, not only because it combines the best features and style of many different conveyances, but also because no single part of it will ever wear out. This extraordinary building tech-

* See *Ozma of Oz*, by L. Frank Baum.

nique was discovered by Mr. Smith, with whom I had the honor and privilege of working. Mr. Smith, as you may know, was not only an excellent inventor and an outstanding machinist, but was also the finest painter who ever lived.

"Just a short time after Mr. Smith's unfortunate drowning, Mr. Tinker made his trip to the moon, and I was left as engineer in charge of the factory. During this period the Nome King, who had previously contracted for and received several mechanical marvels from the firm, approached me and asked for a number of machines which could do both pick and shovel work, and also, on command, rake and spade.

"I was somewhat apprehensive about doing business with this Nome King, and so I asked him why, when he had millions of nomes to do his bidding, he needed these machines?

"He gave me an equivocal answer, and when I pressed him further he grew quite enraged and told me to do as I was told without question. He further stated that if I did not have a model of the machine ready within one week it would be the worse for me. With that remark the Nome King left the building.

"He had, however, left one of his nome courtiers to watch me and see that I carried out his instructions. This nome was exceedingly disagreeable, and rarely spoke without a sneer or jibe. One remark, which he inadvertantly let drop, was that the Nome King intended to use the machines to dig the rare and precious metals and stones from the earth, while he organized all the nomes—who were no longer needed to work the mines—into soldiers in his army. With these soldiers he intended to conquer the earth and take back from the 'hateful earth crawlers' all the valuable jewels and metals they had 'stolen' from his realm.

The Red Wagon

"It was because of King Roquat the Red's threat that I decided to emigrate. So I borrowed Mr. Tinker's first experimental ladder and made my way across the Deadly Desert to the Land of OZ."

"How in the world were you able to cross the Deadly Desert?" asked Ozma.

"It was not at all difficult for one who had Mr. Tinker's astonishing telescoping ladder," said Mr. Wainwright. "First I made my way from Evna to the edge of the Deadly Desert, where I waited for a suitable cloud to pass over. Waiting was the difficult part for there are few clouds over the desert and fewer yet which are being blown eastward toward the Land of OZ. I was also worried lest the Nome King should discover that I had fled and send his minions to find me. So I waited on the edge of the Deadly Desert—a place given over to solitude, silence and desolation.

"Looking on it one sees only miles and miles of bottomless sand and alkali, sparsely covered with a carpet of small sun-bleached stones. The heat is indescribable. In places huge out-croppings of rock emerge like fractured bones. There are no trees, no shrubs, no shade. There is no color – only gray. In some places poisonous alkali dust rises in thick choking clouds and hangs as a pall across the face of the desert. In other places the rising dust and wind combine to form dancing devils of heat which whirl across the desert. Life as we know it, Princess, cannot exist in the Deadly Desert.

"Finally, a small cloud which was being blown eastward, appeared. As it began to pass over me I emplanted the base of the ladder firmly in the ground, stepped on the first rung and pulled with my hands. This action caused the ladder to extend higher and higher until it finally nudged against the cloud. Once on the cloud, I got off the ladder, telescoped it back to its original size and waited until the cloud drifted over the Deadly Desert to the Land of OZ.

"I again emplanted the ladder firmly on the cloud, stepped onto it and pushed. The ladder descended and when it reached the ground, I got off, collapsed the ladder and stowed it in my pack.

"Upon my safe arrival, I took my foot in hand and began my travels in search of a place where I wanted to live. After wandering for some time, first in the Golden West, and then through Rosewood Meadows, I found this town. The name of the town, Wagon Gap, and the name of my trade, wagon maker, seemed more than coincidental, so here I settled and here I hope to remain."

"And so you shall, so you shall," rejoined the mayor. "That is if it's all right with you, Princess Ozma," he added hastily.

"Of course," said Ozma, "you are welcome to stay here forever, and I hope that you will always be happy and contented. Now tell me about the other people who worked for Smith and Tinker. Won't the Nome King take revenge on them?"

The Red Wagon

"No, Your Majesty," replied Wainwright, "King Roquat knows that I was the only one who had the knowledge needed to manufacture his machines, therefore, he has no reason to harm the other employees. Since the drowning of King Evoldo and the enchantment of the royal family, and because there is no one in Ev able to defy him, he is already all-powerful in that land.

"Ev is now being ruled by a coterie of some ten or fifteen princesses, all named Langwidere, who seem more concerned with admiring their pretty faces than with helping their subjects. This is a very strange situation and one that I do not fully understand.

"Now, with your permission Princess, I will tell you of your Red Wagon," continued Dcim Wainwright, "In an ordinarily built cart or wagon there is always a weak spot somewhere. There is none in this wagon. That, I promise you. All the craftmen and I have ensured that the hubs, tires, panels, felloes, crossbars and the thoroughbrace are made of the strongest oak, the straightest ash, and the toughest elm. So we can truly say:

> 'The wheels are just as strong as the thills,
> The floor as strong as the sills,
> The panels are just as strong as the floors,
> The whifletrees neither less nor more,
> And the back crossbar just as strong as the fore.'*

"It will last you a thousand years Princess, for it also has love built in it, and love is the strongest force there is. Please accept it with our sincere wishes that you will always ride in it in happiness."

At this point the beautiful Red Wagon, drawn by the Sawhorse, preceded by the village band and followed by a noisy group of boys and girls and dogs, made its appearance. My, how it gleamed in the sun, and my, how the assembled people cheered! Some cheered for the Red Wagon and its troupe, but more cheered for Ozma, who was now standing. The

* *The Deacon's Masterpiece* or *The Wonderful "One-Hoss Shay"*
by Oliver Wendell Holmes

glowing emerald-green cushions and pads contrasted colorfully with the shining red of the bodywork. The hubs and axles of electrum, to the power and strength of triple steel, blazed in the sunlight, and the whiffletrees. glistened with polish. On both sides sparkled the royal emblem of OZ. It was altogether a breathtaking sight.

"Now I must make a speech," Ozma thought to herself. "What can I say that will even partly express my gratitude? I can only tell them that I love and cherish them all, and that I will try to rule with wisdom, sympathy and gentleness rather than with fear, cruelty and senselessness. I will tell them that I do not know everything and will make some mistakes and, therefore, I depend on them to help me to understand their problems as well as to forgive me my errors."

And that is exactly what she told them, ending with, "Thank you all for this beautiful gift and for the love which accompanies it. Also, I have this for you," she said, smiling mischievously at Dcim Wainwright. With that she stepped to his side and, standing on her tip-toes, kissed him roundly on the cheek—much to his surprise and confusion.

And, if you think that there was cheering and noise before, you should have heard the din which this action caused. Even the dogs entered fully into the spirit of the occasion and almost turned themselves inside out with their barking.

In the midst of this hubbub, Ozma, nearly overcome with emotion, ran forward, knelt in the dust, took the Sawhorse's head in her hands and choked out:

"Thank you, Sawhorse, for being so thoughtful."

Then rising, she said to all the people, "Thank you again, loyal subjects. Goodbye to you all."

And with that the Sawhorse trotted out of the village, pulling the Red Wagon, with a happy little girl, who waved to all from her wonderful Red Wagon.

Chapter 16

Mister Mocker

he two adventurers soon rejoined the oyster shell road and the Sawhorse said, "Princess, I mean Tip, let us see if that man made as good a wagon as he claimed. Hang on! I am going to run."

When the Sawhorse said run, he meant just that. Although small, with thin legs, he had tremendous strength, and not being made of flesh and bone, he was never tired. It only took him a few seconds to reach top speed and there at his tireless gait he effortlessly pulled the Red Wagon. The wagon ran smoothly without a squeak, creak or rattle. The landscape flashed by so fast that the trees were just a blur. Ozma, exuberant with happiness and excitement, took off her phrygian cap and let her hair stream in the wind. They went so fast that the wheels hardly touched the ground. Dcim Wainwright had told no lie when he said that the Red Wagon was the finest conveyance since the 'One Hoss Shay.'

Ozma was almost limp from excitement when she pulled on the reins in an effort to slow the Sawhorse down. Nothing happened, so she tugged harder, and finally tugged so hard that she pulled the Sawhorse's head up. Then he slowed down, turned his head, and rolled one knotty eye at her, questioningly.

"That is better," Ozma said, "let's slow down for a while, I want to put my cap back on and be Tip again. You have proved that you can pull the Red Wagon and it has proved that it can be pulled."

"Tip," said the Sawhorse, sharply, "I do not know what you want me to do. You tug on the reins for me to slow down and you make those 'gitty-up' sounds for me to go faster."

"I did not make any sounds at all," Tip exclaimed. "All I did was pull on the reins to slow you down. And then just a moment ago I remembered that you did not know what that meant. Now I find out that you do understand the use of reins. Who told you about them? Mr. Wainwright?" Tip asked curiously. "You do not need reins for you understand perfectly anything anyone tells you."

"No, Mr. Wainwright did not tell me," replied the Sawhorse. "It was that foolish Woggle-Bug, I mean Professor Woggle-Bug. He told me in that arrogant way of his that real horses had reins as a badge of office, and that I could not consider myself a real horse until I had reins and understood the use of them. He should see me now."

But there was little chance of that, for H.M. Woggle-Bug, T.E. was deep in his plans to establish a University of OZ — with himself as president and chancellor.

Some little time back, when Ozma was really Tip, she, the Sawhorse, the Scarecrow and the Tin Woodman had met a most extraordinary bug. It was a Woggle-Bug, but no ordinary Woggle-Bug. It had lived for some time in a schoolroom and there had been discovered by the teacher. By means of an enlarger he had magnified the bug to its present size — which was about the size of a normal man. His size and the learning he had absorbed while in the schoolroom gave him his title: Highly Magnified Woggle-Bug, Thoroughly Educated. His supercilious manner and his habit

of making puns had not endeared him to the Sawhorse.

Tip tucked her hair back into her cap, and disregarding Sawhorse's comment about the Woggle-Bug, said, "Sawhorse, I did not urge you on. I wonder who did?"

"Lefty," said a voice from under the Red Wagon.

"Lefty! Who in the world is Lefty?" Tip and the Sawhorse exclaimed, and they both looked under the wagon.

"I am Lefty," said a large gray and black bird, who seemed to be mostly legs, tail and beak. He might have been considered ugly if it were not for the beautiful rainbows under his eyes.

"I am one of the fastest runners in the world and I can outrun any horse that ever existed, let alone a horse pulling a wagon. But that thing . . ." at this point he strutted out from under the wagon and contemplated the Sawhorse, critically, "Certainly can run," he finished. "What do you call it?" he asked Tip. "Even a creature as ugly and ungainly as that must have a name. Tell me what it is."

"Oh, he has a name all right," answered Tip, a little nettled at the bird's bad manners. "He is the Sawhorse, and besides being the fastest and most tireless horse there is, he has another distinctive trait." "Then Tip warned, "Lefty, watch your toes!"

And Lefty did. And just in time too, for the Sawhorse made a good try at stamping on the bird's toes.

"All right, you two, that is enough," Tip ordered. "No more unkind remarks from you Mr. Bird, and please do not crush his toes, Sawhorse.

"Tell me," Tip addressed the bird, "exactly what kind of a bird are you? Most birds I have seen live in trees and in the meadows, not on the roads."

"First," said the bird, "tell me your name. Tip? Very well Tip, I will tell you. I am a roadrunner and I live on the ground – not in trees. My home is in Mudge, where there are few trees, but there were none at all in my previous home. That was the Great Sandy Waste, before it was changed into the Deadly Desert by some officious fairy, and I was forced to leave.

"I have wings and can fly, but I prefer to run along the sand dunes or roads and catch lizards with my strong, tough beak. Fat, succulent lizards – ah, they make a feast fit for a king. have you ever eaten lizard, Tip?" inquired the roadrunner.

Tip shuddered. "No," he exclaimed, "and I do not intend to try, thank you. By the way," Tip asked, hurriedly, trying to change the subject, "how did you get the name of Lefty?"

"Actually, I named myself," exclaimed Lefty. "I took that name because whenever I raced with anyone I always left him in my dust. I just wish that I had time enough to race that Sawhorse of yours. I would certainly teach him a few things about running. But I must be moving along. I have been away from Mudge for about a month and I am getting hungry. I have not eaten a tasty lizard in all that time. So goodbye to you, Tip, and goodbye to you, slowpoke," he told the Sawhorse, then stretching out his long neck in front and his longer tail in back, away he went.

"If I was not pulling this wagon I would show that smart aleck bird what running really is," muttered the Sawhorse as he trotted down the road.

They had not traveled more than a few yards when Tip heard music coming from a grove of trees to the right of the road. "Hark," he said, "Stop! Listen."

The Sawhorse stopped, cocked his ears toward the sound and they both listened. They heard a song — and what a wonderful song it was — sung by an unseen bird. Everytime the bird opened his mouth there poured out from his throat such music as Tip had never before heard. He sat, rapt, transfixed by the heavenly strains.

Then the song stopped and a bird appeared, then another and finally several more. Some perched on Tip's shoulders and some on the dash-board of the wagon. They chirped and cheeped, fluttered their wings, pecked gently at Tip's ear and tugged at the wisps of hair which escaped from his cap.

"Are you hungry or just friendly?" asked Tip, and the birds replied with a chorus of twitters, warbles and peeps.

"I do not understand bird talk," Tip said, "but I would think that all that chatter means that you are hungry." So he took from his pocket the two seed cakes, given him by Evelita, and crumbled them up for the birds to eat.

Then a thought struck him, and he asked, "Why don't you answer me? I know you can talk. Don't you want to talk?"

A blue jay, gorgeous in his white trimmed sky-blue suit and his smart blue crest, looked at Tip with his bright little eyes, then answered.

"We do not want to talk. We birds have decided that there is entirely too much talking in the land as it is, and not enough singing. So we, most of us that is, have decided that we will sing and not talk and in that way bring pleasure instead of boredom. Besides some of us sing much better than we talk. Don't you agree?" he asked in a harsh voice.

Mister Mocker

The blue jay was certainly not referring to himself when he said that some of the birds sang better than thay talked, for the jay has the worst singing voice of any of the birds, and even his speaking voice is harsh and rasping.

"I certainly agree with you," Tip said, remembering the mayor of Wagon Gap and his speeches. "And speaking of singing, who was singing those marvelous melodies I heard just a few moments ago?"

"That was Mr. Mocker, the mockingbird, who is also known in some places as the nightingale or the bulbul. He has a very beautiful voice but is very modest and retiring. As soon as he noticed that you had stopped and were watching him, he immediately stopped singing. Would you care to meet him? I can fly over there and bring him back with me."

"Oh, please do!" exclaimed Tip. "I want so much to meet him and hear him sing again."

So off flew the blue jay.

He had hardly flown away, and the birds surrounding Tip had hardly finished off the seed cakes, when a big black crow appeared. He elbowed and shouldered his way along the dashboard, pushing the other smaller birds out of his way, until he perched directly in front of Tip.

"My name is Kuskar," the crow croaked, tunelessly, "and I see that I have come too late to have any cake. My greedy friends have eaten it all up. Oh well, it was probably stale, anyhow." Then he asked Tip, rudely, "Who are you, son? Where do you come from and what do you want?"

175

Tip overlooked his bad manners and answered his questions, courteously.

"So you are from Emerald City, are you?" rasped the crow. "I don't suppose you have ever met a scarecrow who I understand lives there now, have you? Farmer Crofter made him to try to frighten us crows away from his corn. I saw through his scheme at once of course, and told the other crows that they had nothing to fear from such a straw dummy. A little girl lifted him down from his pole and they went off along the yellow brick road together. I never saw him again and I do not suppose he ever amounted to anything.

"Well, if there is nothing to eat," he grumbled, "I guess I will be flying off. Try to be more considerate next time, boy, and save some crumbs for latecomers." And with that parting shot he flew off.

"Is Kuskar telling the truth about the scarecrow?" asked a meadowlark, who was perched on Tip's shoulder. "He tells so many fibs that we never know what to believe."

"Some of what he said about the Scarecrow was true," Tip said, "but what that crow did not know was that the Wizard of OZ gave the Scarecrow a large portion of bran-new brains and now the Scarecrow is acknowledged as one of the wisest personages in all OZ. He has had many adventures, both with Dorothy and with me. He was also at one time the ruler of OZ, so he is not as unimportant as that crow imagines."

Back flew the jay, accompanied by a medium sized bird, who wore a coat of modest gray—touched with white. He seemed very shy and bashful, almost ill at ease, as the blue jay introduced him.

"Princess Ozma, may I present Mr. Mocker, who is our finest singer. Mr. Mocker," he added sternly, "make your bow to our ruler, and don't be so shy."

Mister Mocker

The little gray bird bobbed his head once or twice, looked at Ozma, and tried to speak to her. But try as he might, his shyness was too over-powering and he could not utter a single word.

Ozma was surprised at the jay's references to her title and asked him, "How did you know that I am Princess Ozma? The Sawhorse and I have kept that secret most of the time."

"I am sorry if I spoke out of turn," said Cy, Cy being short for Cyanurus, which is the bluejay's full name. "But a little while ago a thrush flew by on his way to Glinda's palace and told us that the ruler of OZ, disguised as a boy and riding in a red wagon, was just leaving Wagon Gap. We would have been dull birds, indeed, if we had not recognized you. We may choose to be mute but we are not dumb."

It was at precisely this instant that Mr. Mocker dipped his head, chirped a single note and flew away.

"Oh, I am sorry that he went away," said Ozma, "I was looking for-ward to listening to some more of his superb singing."

"Don't fret Princess, I am certain that he will return in just a mo-ment," said the blue jay.

And sure enough in just a moment the mocking-bird returned, carrying in his beak a tightly closed primrose bud. He dropped it in Ozma's lap and watched her closely as she pinned the bud to the front of her coat. As soon as she had done this the bud opened into a lustrous flower, radiating color.

Mr. Mocker chirped something to the jay, who then said, "Mr. Mocker says that because a primrose will only radiate in that manner when worn by either a good fairy or another blameless being, he now knows for certain that you are the Princess Ozma, and that as his ruler you will not do anything to harm him. So with your permission he will perch on the front of your wagon and serenade you with all the songs he knows.

"We all know," continued the jay, "that as ruler of OZ you have dominion over all creatures, all things for that matter—both vital and inert. We know that having dominion over us you can do anything you want to do to us. But even though we are small and helpless in the face of your power, we have no reason to fear you, because we know that you are honorable and true.

"We are all your subjects, all living things, and we know that we will receive from you justice, understanding and love. We know that you know the more power one has the gentler one will be toward those who have little or no power. You also are only a member of the entire brotherhood of life and know that cruelty and brutality from one member toward another is unthinkable. We know you know these things and that this knowledge is the foundation of your rule. That is why we all flew to meet you. And besides," the jay added mischievously, "no one but a princess would give us all the seed cakes that were supposed to be a snack for her."

Ozma's gratitude shone in her eyes and the gray and white bird perched himself on the wagon, threw back his head and sang. And lord, how he sang! Minutes melted away as the deliciously pure notes— the trills, warbles and croons filled the afternoon air with their glory. There was no other sound, even the Sawhorse stood spellbound as the mockingbird's marvelous music gushed forth from his throat.

Finally he stopped and there was a moment of awe—until Ozma shook herself and returned to reality.

"Mr. Mocker," she whispered, "that was the most glorious singing I have ever heard. Thank you very much. You are indeed, the best loved of all the birds."

"I wish I had a nice voice like that," murmured the jay humbly.

"Now, now, Mr. Blue Jay, don't be envious," chided Ozma gently. "Mr. Mocker has the most beautiful voice but you have the most beautiful apparel. Your are both equally blessed," she smiled warmly. "I must leave you now and be on my way to Glinda's. Goodbye and thank you, thank you all again."

"I am sorry you must leave us, Princess," said the blue jay sadly, "but I and all the others are happy that we were able to meet you, even for such a short time. So God-speed and may you enjoy the rest of your trip, but remember to beware of the Hill of the Hammerheads—you had better plan to go around it.

"Your path now lies through the rest of this majestic forest, which is ruled by a gigantic lion—who some say is a great coward. This I do not know, but I doubt it for there is none in the forest that dares dispute his word. Again, goodbye and good luck to you both," cried the jay as the Sawhorse pulled the Red Wagon along the road which led into the heart of the forest.

Chapter 17

Tip Names The Hungry Tiger

 awhorse, please stop here," Ozma requested, and the Sawhorse complied, halting the Red Wagon in the very center of the oyster shell road.

"This must surely be the forest where the Scarecrow and the Tin Woodman said that the Cowardly Lion rules. See the difference between this forest and that other neglected one we entered? There are just as many trees here and just as much foliage, but here the forest is cool and shady, not cold and gloomy. Here the underbrush is under control, not running riot; here there is a warmth and coziness as the sunlight filters down through the trees; here the birds are singing, and look, there is a doe and her fawn. And the fragrance of this woodland is so lovely — the perfume of the cedars and pines, and that hearty, earthy odor of the ground. Ozma paused for a moment, then said tenderly, "Poor little Sawhorse, you miss so much by having no sense of smell."

The Sawhorse started forward slowly and the two forged deeper into the woods, both exclaiming at the beauty of this primeval forest. Then in a reply to a question asked by the Sawhorse, Ozma replied .

"No, I do not intend to talk to either the trees or the Dryad of this forest. I only want to meet the Cowardly Lion."

At this moment the underbrush beside the road shook and quivered as an immense lion, who was hidden in the bushes, exclaimed to his companion, "Did that boy say he was going to beat me? Why would he want to beat me? I never did anything to him. Beat me, indeed."

The lion's companion, an equally huge tiger also concealed in the bushes, declared impatiently, "He didn't say beat you, he said *meet* you, and he will shortly get his wish or I am badly mistaken."

These two beasts had heard the approach of the Red Wagon from deep in the forest, and out of curiosity and hunger had made their way rapidly and noiselessly through the trees to the edge of the oyster shell road. There they lay in ambush awaiting the approach of Ozma and the Sawhorse. One of these animals was the King of the Forest—the Cowardly Lion—who was impelled by curiosity rather than hunger, and the other was his best friend and councillor, a beautiful striped tiger, who claimed to be always hungry. Neither Ozma nor the Sawhorse even suspected the presence of these two enormous beasts.

Sitting in the Red Wagon, Ozma, enthralled by the beauty of the forest, and by the antics of a family of squirrels in a nearby tree, asked the Sawhorse to stop for a moment. He did and the Red Wagon halted directly in front of the place where the Cowardly Lion and his tiger friend were concealed in the underbrush.

"What did he say? What did the boy say this time?" querilously quizzed the lion of his companion.

"Shh," enjoined the tiger, "not so loud or they will hear you. What is the matter with you? Can't you hear what people say anymore?"

"I am sorry, but my heart is pounding so hard that I can't hear very well," whispered the lion. "It is terrible to be so cowardly."

"Well, gather up your courage and let's have a belated luncheon or early dinner, whichever you prefer. You take the horse and I will take the boy. Let's go!"

"No, wait!" exclaimed the Cowardly Lion, "You can eat the horse if you want and I will punish the boy."

"You are bigger than I, and stronger too," said the tiger. "You eat the horse and I will eat the boy."

"NO! I said for you to eat the horse if you want. You are hungrier than I and the horse is bigger than the boy. Furthermore I am the king and I order you to obey me. Besides the boy said he wanted to beat me and I wish to punish him for that—not eat him. I could never eat up a young child," concluded the lion.

"I told you that he said 'meet you' not 'beat you'," sighed the tiger. "But all right, if that is the way you want it that is the way it will be. Now get ready and at the count of three we will spring. One, two, three," counted the tiger, and sprang.

The sharp ears of the Sawhorse heard the rustle of the underbrush, and out of the corner of his eye he caught a glimpse of the tiger just as the tiger was beginning to leap. The sawhorse immediately pulled himself partly free of his traces and lashed out with his gold shod hooves. He kicked the tiger right under the chin and knocked him unconscious.

Tip Names The Hungry Tiger

As the tiger fell in a heap at the sawhorse's feet the Cowardly Lion gave a tremendous roar and sprang at Ozma, who immediately leaped to her feet and cried out, "Stop, Cowardly Lion, stop! I am Ozma of OZ."

The Cowardly Lion heard her call out, and, as her cry registered in his mind, he attempted to stop his attack. Already in mid-air he could not stop, but he was able to twist his huge body sideways and change direction. This was unfortunate, for this change of direction caused him to land with a thud right on top of the prostrate tiger. Unable to maintain either footing or balance, he stumbled right into the Sawhorse. That short-tempered one, always vexatious and irascible, began to kick the lion unmercifully and the Cowardly Lion, now completely disconcerted, took to his heels, leaving the Sawhorse undisputed master of the field.

These actions had taken place so fast that Ozma had no time to be frightened. The sudden appearance of the tiger and the roar of the lion had startled her of course, but the rapidity with which the Sawhorse had dispatched the tiger and caused the lion to retreat so cravenly reassured her that she was in no danger. Now she was certain that the lion was indeed the friend of the Scarecrow and the Tin Woodman — the Cowardly Lion.

Tip Names The Hungry Tiger

"Wait, Cowardly Lion," she called out. "Please don't run! I want to talk with you. The Scarecrow and the Tin Woodman have told me so much about you that I feel we are already friends."

The Cowardly Lion, who had been more startled than frightened by the turn of events with the Sawhorse, stopped on hearing Ozma's call, turned and regarded the passenger of the Red Wagon with new interest and undisguised admiration.

"That is not a boy," he thought. "There is not a boy alive with hair like that." For Ozma had taken off her cap and allowed her long golden hair to stream in the breeze. "Perhaps she really is the ruler of OZ," he mused.

Seeing his friend the tiger lying unconscious on the ground, he trotted back to where Ozma stood beside her faithful Sawhorse.

"Not too close, you overgrown tomcat," warned the Sawhorse, "or I will do to you what I did to your friend."

The Cowardly Lion stared at the wooden horse with mixed amusement and respect, and said, "Don't push your luck too far my wooden friend, for if I become really angry with you I will smash you into a pile of kindling. But I do not want to do that to such a brave creature. You are the only other creature beside me who ever overcame my friend, the tiger."

"Both of you stop this bickering, it is not seemly," Ozma commanded, and the two beasts fell silent.

"You, she addressed the lion, "are you really the famous Cowardly Lion, the friend of the Scarecrow, the Tin Woodman and Dorothy Gale of Kansas? If you are, I am very happy to meet you because the Scarecrow and Tin Woodman have told me so many tales of your bravery and chivalry."

"Maybe they both exaggerated a little about my prowess, but I am the Cowardly Lion, and I am very pleased to meet you. But tell me, are you really Princess Ozma, or just a boy with long hair?"

Here the Sawhorse interrupted, "That 'boy with long hair' is in fact the Ruler of OZ and all who are in it. And that includes you, you long haired pussy cat. So make your obeisance to your ruler."

"That piece of scrap kindling has a very sharp tongue and someday it will get him into more trouble than he bargained for," observed the Cowardly Lion. "However, as I recognize you as the Princess Ozma, I pledge you my love and allegiance and I want you to know that I will always defend you to the utmost of my ability. And I can also guarantee the loyalty of my friend the tiger, who I see is beginning to stir."

And the tiger *was* beginning to stir. The huge striped beast had opened his eyes and was groggily trying to get to his feet when he caught sight of the Sawhorse glaring malevolently at him. This worked its magic and with a coughing roar the tiger sprang to his feet and snarlingly gazed at the Sawhorse, his cold yellow eyes reflecting hate.

"Hold on, my tigerish friend," warned the lion. "Don't do anything rash. These are friends and the boy is the Princess of OZ to whom I have just sworn allegiance. Don't start any trouble."

"Stand back Your Majesty," the tiger said to the Cowardly Lion, "I do not care who the boy is, but I am going to chew that so-called horse into toothpicks. No one or no thing kicks me around like that without paying for it." And with that remark he crouched to spring.

"I am sorry to have to do this," said the Cowardly Lion regretfully,

Tip Names The Hungry Tiger

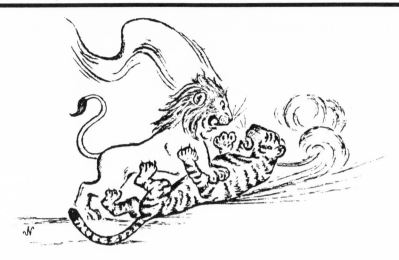

"but duty is duty." And with this he pounced on the tiger, rolled him over and with his great mouth on the tiger's throat asked, "Must I punish you further or will you obey me? The Sawhorse did nothing but protect himself and if you just calm down and think for a moment you will realize that he is a very brave and strong creature and will make you and me a much better friend than an enemy. In any case, the girl, who says she is not a boy — but looks like one — and that Sawhorse are not to be touched! Do you understand?"

"I understand," replied the tiger. "You are right about the Sawhorse, and I was wrong, so I apologize. But I still do not understand who the long haired boy is, or how a boy can be the Princess of OZ. You might let me up and explain that."

As the Sawhorse watched closely, the Cowardly Lion moved aside and the tiger got to his feet, stretched, then crouched to listen to the lion's explanation. Ozma, with a smile on her face, also prepared to listen.

"I will explain the entire situation to you in simple terms. To begin with, the boy in the Red Wagon is not a boy at all, but he knows the Scarecrow and the Tin Woodman — I mean *she* does. And he is also Princess Ozma of OZ, I mean she is. But when he travels, or rather she travels . . . "

Tip Names The Hungry Tiger

"Wait, Cowardly Lion," Ozma laughingly interrupted, "let me explain it to him. Hungry Tiger, for that will be your name from now on, I am Princess Ozma of OZ, the ruler of this entire land. I am a girl, but I am traveling incognito, dressed as a boy."

"Incognito means without anyone knowing who she is," whispered the lion to the Hungry Tiger.

"I know what it means," retorted the tiger irritably, "and I know it also means no lunch for us today."

He then addressed Ozma, "Princess we have all heard of you, and we all admire and love you very much. If I had known who you were at the onset I would never have allowed the Cowardly Lion to talk me into attacking you. Therefore, please accept my apologies and my undying devotion and allegiance."

Ozma smiled to herself at the masterly way in which the Hungry Tiger had shifted all the blame for the attack onto the Cowardly Lion's shoulders, and almost broke out into laughter at the expression on the lion's face. But she said soberly, "Thank you both for your pledges of loyalty. I accept them gratefully and hope that we will be able to see much more of each other in the future. It would also please me very much if you two and my Sawhorse would make up. You three should be fast friends instead of enemies. Will you please?"

The Sawhorse, with one backward look at Ozma, took the initiative. He walked up to the Cowardly Lion and extended his stiff right foreleg and shook paws—hooves, and then turned and touched noses with the Hungry Tiger.

"If the princess accepts you, then I want to be your friend, for I feel that we can better serve her as friends than as enemies," he said.

Tip Names The Hungry Tiger

"Well said, well said, friend," exclaimed both the Cowardly Lion and the Hungry Tiger, and with these statements the tension seemed to lift and the air became clearer.

Now that amity had been established, Ozma was able to get a better look at the two beasts of the forest. The Cowardly Lion's immense golden body was set off by a heavy brown mane, and his powerful legs ended in massive paws equipped with long, sharp talons. His amber colored eyes were clear and friendly, but his mouthful of long sharp teeth seemed not so friendly. His noble carriage proclaimed him every inch a king—honorable and magnanimous.

The Hungry Tiger's sinewy, yellow colored body with its startling contrast of black stripes was equally long as the lion's, but not so massive. His fur, though, was thicker and softer, as Ozma discovered as she stroked the great beast's neck, and heard his rumbling purring. His head seemed almost too large for his body, and his eyes, although clear and direct, lacked the imperiousness of the Cowardly Lion's.

They were both magnificent beasts.

"Cowardly Lion, please tell me something about your adventures. The Scarecrow and the Tin Woodman told me that you asked Glinda the Good for permission to return to this forest, and she ordered the Winged Monkeys to carry you here. What happened after that?"

The Cowardly Lion shuffled his feet and looked embarrassed at Ozma's question, so the Hungry Tiger spoke up. "Princess, let me tell you the story. He is too shy and bashful, even though he is the greatest king this forest, or any other forest for that matter, ever had.

"I presume that this scarecrow has told you how our king, and my best friend, overcame the tremendous monster that was terrorizing our beautiful forest. That great spider-like creature's body was as large as an elephant's and covered with coarse black hair. Its eight legs were as long and thick as tree trunks, its mouth had a double row of sharp teeth a foot long, and the claws on the end of its eight legs were curved and as sharp as scimitars.

"Our king knocked off the creature's head with a single blow of his paw and then watched the body as it squirmed and wriggled, looking for its head. Only when he was satisfied that it could do no more harm did he leave it. Later, one of the squirrels, who had watched the fight, told us that the monster's body and head grew smaller and smaller as time went on, until, when it finally found and rejoined its head to its body, it was no larger than an ordinary, harmless little spider. It now lives in the forest and spins the most beautiful webs I have ever seen, and holds no grudge against the Cowardly Lion."

At this point the Cowardly Lion took up the story : "Destroying the monster was no great deed. My real challange came when I returned and began to rule the forest. I had some trouble with other lions, and tigers and bears, and also with the kalidahs, but I was able to impose my rule with the help and guidance of my Chief Councillor – my friend whom you have named the Hungry Tiger. That name is very apt Princess, for he simply cannot seem to get enough to eat, and what he does eat does not satisfy his hunger pangs for long. He says that the only thing which would stay his appetite would be to eat fat babies. He says that he thinks if he could have a half dozen or so of them, his appetite would be appeased."

"Oh! How terrible!" exclaimed Ozma, "you must never eat a fat baby, or any baby for that matter. That is very wrong. You have not eaten one yet, have you?" she asked anxiously.

"No," replied the tiger. "Unfortunately I also have a very active conscience and that conscience will not allow me this pleasure, so I have never eaten one, and never will. Although I must admit, the thought of a succulent fat baby is very mouth watering." Here the Hungry Tiger opened his great mouth in a yawn and closed it with a snap of teeth.

Ozma looked at him narrowly, then smiled. "I think that you are a big fraud and not half as much of a vicious bully as you pretend. I do not think you would eat a baby under any circumstances, so there."

As the Hungry Tiger smiled slyly behind a paw at the accuracy of this conclusion, the Cowardly Lion abruptly changed the subject.

"Princess, please tell us what happened outside this forest. The only things I have heard was that Dorothy was finally able to return to her home in the United States of Northern America, that the Scarecrow was King of OZ for awhile, and that finally you became ruler. There must have been many other interesting happenings, so please tell us about them."

So Ozma related to the two beasts all the adventures she and others had experienced, including some that even the Sawhorse had not heard about.

"Has anyone seen that humbug Wizard since he flew away in a balloon?" asked the Cowardly Lion.

"No one," answered Ozma. "We never met, you know, and yet I have the strangest feeling that I have known him somewhere."

"His departure is no loss," said the lion. "He was nothing but a fraud as far as I am concerned. The Scarecrow was smart before he got those 'bran new' brains, and the Tin Woodman did not need a heart— he was born tender hearted. But me! That bowl of Filboid Studge he gave me—calling it courage—was worthless. I was born a coward, and a coward I shall remain. Even as King of the Forest I am so cowardly that I am afraid the other animals will find out about it, so I fight fiercely and pretend not to be afraid, isn't that right, Hungry?"

"If you say so, Milord," replied the tiger, "but it seems to me that what you call cowardice is in reality exceptional bravery. You have courage enough to recognize fear and overcome it."

"Well, in any case I miss the Scarecrow and the Tin Woodman and all the others in Emerald City, for now that Hungry and I have established order in the forest there is little of interest to do, and I am bored most of the time," said the Cowardly Lion.

"If that is the case," interjected Ozma, "why don't you leave your tiger friend here as King of the Forest and come and live in Emerald City? I would love to have you, and I know all the others would too."

"I would like that!" declared the Cowardly Lion, and his eyes sparkled in anticipation. Then they clouded.

"I would not leave my friend behind, so I cannot go." he said sorrowfully. Then after a pause, added, "I could go, that is we could go, if you would also invite the Hungry Tiger."

"Why certainly he can come if he wants to," said Ozma. "I would love to have both of you with me. But what will happen to the forest with both of you gone?"

"Please excuse me, your Majesty, while I summon one of my chief councillors," said the Cowardly Lion. He then let out such a roar that the ground shook and the trees swayed back and forth. In less time than it takes to tell, a tremendously large kalidah emerged from the trees, inspected the Red Wagon and the Sawhorse suspiciously and then addressed the Cowardly Lion. "What is it that my lord desires?" he asked.

"The Chief Councillor, the Hungry Tiger, and I will be leaving the forest for an indefinite period of time. We are going to visit Emerald City and stay with Princess Ozma as long as she wants us. Therefore, while we are gone I want you to act as regent in my behalf. You will be in complete charge and I will direct the other denizens of the forest to obey you as they would obey me. Do you accept this responsibility?" asked the Cowardly Lion as he gazed steadily into the eyes of the kalidah.

This monstrous beast, with a body like a bear and a head like a tiger—

Tip Names The Hungry Tiger

one of the largest and fiercest of all animals — returned the Cowardly Lion's gaze without flinching, and said, "I will do as Your Majesty desires, and will continue your rule of justice and understanding."

With this statement he bowed to Ozma, sniffed curiously at the Saw-horse and melted back into the forest.

"Princess," said the Sawhorse, "I think it an excellent idea to have the Cowardly Lion and the Hungry Tiger come to Emerald City. They can stay with me and share my stable. It is too big for one and could easily be redecorated to suit their tastes. I would like to have them stay with me so that I could get to know them better."

Ozma gave her approval and the Cowardly Lion and the Hungry Tiger agreed heartily with the plan. Then after bidding Ozma and the Sawhorse goodbye, they went back into the forest for one last council meeting before departing for Emerald City.

Tip Names The Hungry Tiger

Ozma waved to them and as the Sawhorse was cantering along the road leading out of the forest, Ozma said to the Sawhorse reflectively, "I am thinking of the bird's warning about the Hill of the Hammerheads. It seems to me that when the Scarecrow told us about his and the Tin Woodman's adventures with Dorothy, he said that the hill was right at the boundary between Emerald City and Rosewood Meadows, but everyone with whom we have talked say that it is to the south of us and on the way to Glinda's palace. Well, we shall find out soon for it cannot be too far distant now."

And it was not, for even as Ozma spoke the Red Wagon emerged from the forest and Ozma was able to make out a range of hills stretching out directly in front of her.

"Maybe that is the Hill of the Hammerheads up ahead," she exclaimed, and the Sawhorse, noting the tone of her voice, broke into a rapid trot, which kept up for about an hour.

Chapter 18

The Nome King

f this wagon is a sample of Mr. Wainwright's competence, Roquat the Red certainly made a mistake when he drove Wainwright away," the Sawhorse reflected as he trotted down the oyster shell road.

"Sawhorse, it is strange that you should mention King Roquat for I was just thinking of him. Mr. Wainwright said that he would not harm any of the people of Ev, even though he was mad at Mr. Wainwright for running away. I wonder why not?" asked Tip.

"Because the hobgoblins in his realm might prevent him from doing this evil thing," replied the Sawhorse.

"Hobgoblins prevent him from doing evil? What do you mean? Everyone knows that goblins are the nastiest creatures there are, so hobgoblins must be ever so evil!"

"Not so!" declared the Sawhorse. "Of all the sprites goblins are—as you say—the worst. They are much worse than nomes and a little worse than the orcs or trolls. But there is good in all creatures, even in goblins, and when this good becomes more and more evident, goblins become hobgoblins. Hob is the faerie word for good. So a hobgoblin is a good goblin. And there are more of them than one might think, perhaps even enough of them to force a change for the better in King Roquat.

"But there are other sprites or fairies who are good – better than the hobgoblins, and some who are very bad – worse even than goblins. Have you ever heard of the Thills and the Ghorns? I thought not.

"These two families are the select of all subterranean sprites, but there is constant strife between them because the Thills are good and the Ghorns evil. Even though they both live in the omni-terralunar region, where those dwell whose task it is to order the universe, they seldom associate with one another.

"There are occasions, however, when they do mingle and socialize. These times are exceptional, but even the quarrelsome Ghorns tire of squabbling constantly with the Thills, and a type of truce is established. Many, many years ago, when such a truce was in effect, a marriage took place between a royal princess of the Thills and an equally royal prince of the Ghorns."

"How did you learn all about this?" interrupted Tip. "I have never heard of Thills and Ghorns, even though I have heard a lot of things about the Nome King."

"While you were busy learning how to be a princess, I was not idle," retorted the Sawhorse. "I asked many questions and listened to the answers. A unicorn, name of Nicker, told me about the Metal Monarch. He told me that his great, great, great grandparent, who was present during the latter part of the engagement and the subsequent wedding ceremony, told him that it was evident, even then, that the marriage was destined to fail. He believed that the Thill married the Ghorn with the idea that she could change him for the better, and the Ghorn believed that he could change her for the worse. As is usual in cases like this neither succeeded.

"They did succeed in one objective and that objective was the sole reason why those who order the universe established the truce and arranged the marriage in the first place, although neither the Ghorn prince nor the Thill princess realized this. The fruit of their union was to become the ruler of all the subterranean sprites and thus bring order out of the chaos that was plaguing the underground domain and curtailing the deliveries of jewels and precious metals to the omni-terralunar zone.

"The discord in Ev, which is the name of the subterranean realm of the underground sprites, was the result of the continuing discontent between the trolls and the goblins—with the nomes more or less passively standing by awaiting the outcome. The nomes are the most indefatigable workers of all the underground sprites and are the most even tempered and jolly of all—excepting the hobgoblins.

"The trolls, possibly due to their immense size and strength, are slow to anger, but when angered are slower yet to forgive. Their tasks are those which require great strength—such as moving heavy boulders, carrying out loads of gold, silver and platinum ores and operating the vast frunaces and smelters. The goblins, much smaller and more agile, are quick to take offense and also slow to forgive. They can creep or squirm into places too small for the trolls or nomes and bring out precious gems. They also perform the jewel cutting and sizing operations carried out in Ev.

"As is many times the case each thought his work was the most important and that he was doing the hardest and most unpleasant tasks. So there was ill-temper between the trolls and goblins and each attempted to influence the nomes to side with them in their bickering.

The nomes were easily swayed by the pleas and importunities of each party in turn, but were reluctant to join either side. The only point of agreement between the trolls and goblins was that the nomes were the most irritating, hypocritical and devious individuals extant. The only tempering influence was that exercised by the hobgoblins and that was not enough to bring harmony to the strife ridden netherworld.

"As the schism between the trolls and goblins grew larger and each of their efforts to subvert the nomes became more intense, efforts to locate and process the precious stones and metals decreased. This alone was enough to cause concern in all the terra-lunar realms because they are the primary recipients of the gems and metals dug up in the netherworld, and they did not intend to have their supply interrupted. Also, while the sprites were bickering among themselves, surface dwelling mortals were making significant inroads into the stores of these treasures. Any increase in the amount the mortals took resulted in a decrease in the amount the terra-lunar realms would receive, and this would not be tolerated.

"While it was realized that good and bad — as night and day, black and white, Yin and Yang — must co-exist, there should be a steadying influence in order to prevent complete anarchy. Therefore, those who order the universe decided that an overlord of the underground sprites was needed, and they decreed that Yenoh, Princess Royal and daughter of the Apogee of the Thills should wed Yetsan, son of the Grand Nadir of the Ghorns. Their firstborn would be named Roquat the Red and designated Metal Monarch and Emperor of the Underground World. He was to be thoroughly tutored in all aspects of rulership and sent to his realm as soon as possible.

"Neither the trolls nor the goblins were particularly enthusiastic about this action. They realized that, as the only other course of action would be their complete extinction, they had better accept the decision with as good grace as they could muster. This they did, and overtly joined to pledge allegiance to their new ruler. Covertly, however, they held dark and secret councils among themselves, each trying to figure ways and means to bend the new ruler to their way of thinking. This boded ill for any attempts to make the Metal Monarch a just and open ruler.

"Roquat's mother, Princess Yenoh, was tall and slender with ash brown hair and gently lambent eyes. Her voice was soft and her manner unassuming, but as a Thill her will was strong and she was determined that her child would be a force for good. But she failed to take into account the deviousness and general malevolence of the Ghorns.

"Prince Yetsan in contradistinction was a stocky, stumpy young Ghorn with black hair and the blackest kind of eyes, sunk so deep in his face that he seemed to be looking out of caverns. His voice was harsh and his manner domineering, and as a Ghorn he was equally determined that his offspring should be a force for evil. His will was equally as strong as his wife's and he ballasted it by pretending to agree that the child should be raised to be kind and considerate.

"Prince Yetsan, that master of immorality and intrigue finally convinced Princess Yenoh of his sincerity in desiring to raise Roquat in the way of goodness. So Yenoh congratulated herself on her success in converting Yetsan to the path of gentle kindness.

The prince, in order to accomplish his horrid ends, had praised virtue and censured vice in the presence of his wife, but when he was alone with the youngster mocked honor and made infamy appear desirable. In these actions he was aided by all the other Ghorns who secretly encouraged the bad habits Roquat already had, while teaching him other naughtiness to go with them. They had taught him to dissemble — particularly in the presence of his mother — and to wear good manners as a cloak for evil intentions. They taught him to smile and chuckle when he was planning more cruelty and mischief.

"These nasty Ghorns were so successful in their efforts that Princess Yenoh in her innocence agreed that Roquat was completely fitted to be an able ruler of an important region and a credit to his parents. In this she was half right and did not discover the true nature of Roquat until it was too late. He had already ascended the throne.

The Nome King

"Roquat grew to be a man of full habit, but with spindly legs, a darkish-paley complexion, and benignly piercing eyes. The one remarkable thing about him was his hair — salt and pepper in color — and falling almost to his waist. He was always dressed in black and white with the only color coming from his jewels in the several rings he wore on the fingers of both hands. Around his waist he wore a perfectly enormous belt of iridio-platinum studded with gems of the finest water and color. This was his emblem of authority and it possessed certain eerie and potent alchemic powers. It never left his person.

"To ensure the complete and continuing subjugation of Roquat to evil the Ghorns appointed an outwardly presentable yet fundamentally vicious sprite to be his chief advisor, the Royal Chamberlain. This creature had been born a Thill, but had so corrupted himself through a desire for power, that he was even more treacherous and sinful than the Ghorns. This personification of everything vile and degraded continued to influence Roquat in the belief that goodness and gentleness are a weakness which can and should be bullied and taken advantage of at every opportunity.

The Nome King

"There was no need to train Roquat in the art of kingship; his father and the other Ghorns had done that job well. Roquat ruled by fear and punishment and by intriguing secretly with trolls against goblins and with goblins against trolls. He punished, mercilessly, any transgressions by either of them or the hard-working nomes. This resulted in the output of precious stones and metals returning to acceptable levels.

"Roquat also passionately despised and hated the 'horrid earth crawlers' whom he charged with stealing the treasures of his underground empire. He swore that someday he would conquer all the upper-air mortals and return their riches to the depths of the earth.

"This then was Roquat the Red, Metal Monarch, Emperor of the Underground World and King of the Nomes.*

"It was at this time that those who order the universe decided formally to install Roquat as emperor and asked Skanderbeg, the Original Dragon and Lord of all Living Creatures, to attend the ceremony. Skanderbeg in his usual irritable manner declined to attend, stating that he did not consider Roquat—from what he had heard of him—to be worth the trip. However, he said that he would send the Original Unicorn, Monokeros, Lord of all Beasts, in his stead. So Monokeros went and was not impressed by either Roquat or his court.

* At the time Roquat transformed the trolls and goblins into nomes, the Thills demanded that the Lord Chamberlain be recalled and replaced by a Thill named Qualyquo.

The Nome King

"Nicker said that his great, great, great grandparent told him that the Ghorns and the Lord Chamberlain had done their work well and that to all intents and purposes the Nome King is as evil a creature as can be found anywhere, but that deep down inside him the seeds of goodness which his mother emplanted are still present, if quiescent. Monokeros said that he thought it might be possible for someone who is genuinely kind and understanding to touch this inner goodness and cause Roquat to change his ways. He may never become as good as his mother desired but it is possible that he could improve and become someone who is not bad all the time. He then might find a little happiness for only the good can be happy because the bad spend so much of their time bringing unhappiness to others that they have no time to be happy themselves.

"But when Monokeros mentioned goodness and happiness to the Nome King, Roquat grew wild with anger and raged that he was happy the way he was. Then he recklessly threatened that if Monokeros continued to harp on the subject he, Roquat, would become even happier than he was now by punishing Monokeros.

"Monokeros, Lord of All Beasts, laughed in his face and told Roquat that he was certainly not afraid of anything an unimportant netherworld satrap like Roquat might try to do to him. The Nome King realized the uncautiousness of his remark and smiling guiltily said hoarsely that he was just joking.

"In spite of all this, or perhaps because of the way Roquat reacted to his remark, Monokeros believes even more firmly that there is some latent good in the Nome King and that it should be brought out. But he does not think that the few remaining hobgoblins have enough understanding to bring it out."

"Well," said Tip, "that was very interesting. I agree that the hobgoblins probably are not strong enough to force the Nome King to change his ways, and in any case I do not think that the royal family of Ev should be dependent on the hobgoblins for their freedom. I believe that I should try to make the Nome King mind his manners and leave helpless people alone. I may ask the hobgoblins to help, but I think I should attend to this matter in person.

"Sawhorse," continued Tip, "you are a constant source of amazement to me. You know more about what is going on than anyone else in my kingdom."

The Sawhorse smiled to himself at this remark and continued his canter until they arrived at the foot of the range of low hills which stretched far off into the distance both to the left and right.

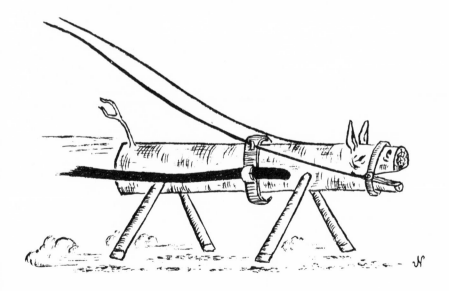

Chapter 19

Descent into The Chasm

he hills were rocky and forbidding, but between the two highest was a cleft which formed a pass through the range. The oyster shell road forked, one branch led off to the right of the hills, while the other – which was probably the original road but was now little more than a rocky path – led up the boulder strewn hillside to the pass. There was no sign of the Hammerheads nor any indication that they lived in this area.

This rocky path was indeed the original road, but after the difficulties the Scarecrow, Tin Woodman and Dorothy Gale of Kansas had with the Hammerheads, Glinda had ordered that a new road be built to bypass the hills.

"This must be the Hill of the Hammerheads," Ozma said, "and apparently the Scarecrow was wrong when he said that the hill was at the edge of the Emerald City area. Well, it was his first trip and he probably became a little mixed up in his locations."

"Perhaps the brains the Wizard gave him were not yet in perfect

Descent into The Chasm

working order," commented the Sawhorse, drily, "because as I remember the story he also said that the forest of fighting trees was in the Emerald City area. Well, as you say, Princess, no matter. But which road shall we take, the low road around the hills or the high road through the pass?"

"We must take the road up the hill to that cleft, because I have the strangest feeling that I am expected to be here. I know, now, that one of the purposes of this trip was to meet with someone here. Please, let's go on up. And you may as well as stop calling me Tip for it seems that everyone in OZ has seen through my masquerade."

The Sawhorse neighed his agreement, turned off the newer road onto the old one and started up the hill.

Descent into The Chasm

They had not proceeded far when a harsh voice on their left cried out, "Keep back!"

The Sawhorse was having a difficult time keeping the Red Wagon in the lane because of the many 'potholes' and generally bad condition of the path. But when he heard the voice he moved as far to the right of the lane as he could, and continued on.

"Keep back!" another harsh voice, this time on the right, warned. But the Sawhorse, who was rapidly losing his temper, broke into a run up the hill.

"Sawhorse, stop!" cried out Ozma. "This is the Hill of the Hammerheads and we must not try to force our way. So please stop."

The plea, however, came too late for from behind a rock stepped the strangest man either of them had ever seen. He was short and stocky and his large head was flat on top and held up by a thick, wrinkled neck. The man leaned over and, just as the Red Wagon was coming to a stop, shot his neck out until the top of his head where it was flat, struck the right front wheel of the Red Wagon and smashed it. Then almost as quickly as his neck had stretched out it snapped back into his body. The wagon tipped over and spilled Ozma out onto the ground. Several other Hammerheads appeared, eyed Ozma closely, leaned over and seemed about to shoot their heads out and hit her, when a deep voice boomed out.

Descent into The Chasm

"HOLD!"

The Hammerheads immediately straightened up and Ozma saw that there were hundreds of them dotting the hillside. They were dressed in varying shades of maroon and rust and when they squatted down behind the rocks and bushes they were very difficult to see. But now they were standing and looking expectantly toward a dolmen on the top of the hill from where the voice seemed to have come.

The voice continued, "Did you not observe the primrose this young girl is wearing? Have you forgotten that the primrose only radiates in that manner when it is worn by one who is under the protection of the Power? Do you defy the law that protects the wearer from harm, or have you another less odious reason for ignoring the law?"

"We were only making sure that no harm came to the sacred haw-thorns," explained one of the Hammerheads.

"So you try to protect the sacred trees by breaking the sacred law? That is wrong and you all know it. Go to your holes."

In a trice all the Hammerheads had disappeared.

Descent into The Chasm

By now Ozma was
on her feet and looking
down at the primrose
she was wearing on her
jacket. It was radiating,
pulsating really, as it changed
colors through the various shades
of red, yellow, white and back again
to red.

The voice again spoke, this time
in a gentler tone.

"Wearer of the fairy flower, please
walk through the avenue of hawthorns
to a cave you will find near the leg of the
dolmen. Enter the cave and follow the
passageway. At its end turn to your left and follow a ledge which will lead
you down to where the Presence is waiting to meet with you, if you are
the one she awaits.

"A warning. You will need the power of the magic flower in order to
gain admittance to where you desire to go. If you are one who can call on
the powers of good, and are not afraid, the primrose will light your way
and keep you from harm. If, however, you are one who can call on evil
powers to camouflage your true nature and so allow you to pass as one
who can command good, beware! The primrose will not help you. It will
not harm you, but it cannot protect you from harm. So think before you
enter the cave because once you have started down the path to the heart
of the hill, there is no turning back.

"I will send someone to remove the broken wheel from your conveyance and have it repaired by its builder. With your permission, my emis-
sary will ride your Sawhorse to and from Wagon Gap with the wheel."

"Creature," the voice addressed the Sawhorse, "do you understand?"

"Yes," the Sawhorse answered.

Descent into The Chasm

"Who is this person, or creature or whatever, who is waiting to talk to me?" asked Ozma. "I am . . . "

The voice interrupted. "It is no part of my business to know your identity. You came, wearing the primrose whose luminescence proves that you are no ordinary individual. My instructions are to show any such being the way to the Presence."

"Don't go, Princess!" exclaimed the Sawhorse. "It may be dark before you come out—if you are able to come out. Unhitch me from this wagon and I will take you away from here. There is something about this hill that is weird and may mean harm. Maybe the flower is evil, not good, and only wants to lead you into some danger. Come, Princess," the Sawhorse pleaded, "please come away with me."

"No," replied Ozma, "there is something here that I must do. I think that is the reason I set out on this trip. You obey the voice. I will be all right. Now I am going in."

With that remark she set out up the hill through the lane bordered by the hawthorns to the foot of the dolmen. Here at this strange rock formation, which resembled a table with three columnar legs, she saw the entrance to the cave. And in the warmth of the late afternoon sun she paused for a moment, looked about her, entered the dimly lit cave and set out down the passageway.

The passageway or tunnel was lined with stones that had obviously been set in place recently and suggested nothing more than makeshift masonry. But commencing about fifty feet inside the cave the tunnel was made of great blocks, carefully squared, and so meticulously placed that the course seemed to be carved out of solid rock. The stones were dry but there was a smell of dampness in the air.

Descent into The Chasm

Ozma made her way through the gloom and finally came upon a slightly raised platform at the end of the tunnel. There she paused and cautiously felt with her foot. There was nothing there. The path had ended and she was standing at the edge of a vast pit, and from that pitch dark hole came such a draft of cold air as to bring shivers to her body. By the faint glow of the primrose Ozma could make out a narrow set of steps, roughly hewn from bare rock, that led off to the left and down into the darkness. The steps were unprotected by even a makeshift handrail. There was no sound.

She hesitated no longer because she knew that if she did not go on at once, her imagination would invent such paralyzing dangers that she would be unable to move. So her will conquered her fears and she began the descent.

She moved cautiously, left arm pressed against the towering rock face and right arm hanging over the sheer drop, always circling downward. The steps were so narrow and the descent so steep that it was impossible to turn around and climb back up. So she went on to face the unknown in the stygian darkness below.

As she made her way down she seemed at times to catch a glimpse of a red pinprick many, many feet below. But she dared not take her eyes from the steps and look directly at this spot of light lest vertigo should overtake her. Fortunately the steps were not slippery so she felt she would not fall unless she grew careless or frightened.

Descent into The Chasm

As she moved cautiously down the ledge, her left side pressing against the wall and her right side bathed with the cold draft of air which came from somewhere at the bottom of the chasm, the fear which she had felt just before she had started down the ledge returned. As that fear grew the glow from the primrose dimmed and as it waned the fear grew. Finally the light from the primrose went out completely; Ozma's right foot slipped and she stumbled forward. Both hands flew to the wall in an effort to keep from falling, but there was no handhold to be found. Fear flooded over her in waves as her hands scrabbled frantically for a hold on the sheer face of the cliff.

With the light of the primrose extinguished Ozma was left struggling for balance in the utter blackness of this huge well. She fell to her knees and as her body swayed perilously on the ledge she remembered the last words the voice had spoken to her before she entered the cave of the dolman.

"If you are not fearful, you cannot be frightened, and if you are not frightened you cannot fall."

As these words came back to her and she understood their meaning, all fear vanished, the glow of the primrose returned and she continued down the rim toward the red pinprick of light — which she could see more distinctly now.

Minutes ticked on interminably as Ozma circled downward. Below her the red pinprick became more distinct and she felt that she was finally reaching the bottom. With wobbly knees and bathed in perspiration she stood beside a red lantern hanging from a sconce in front of a strangely carved curtained stone arch.

She drew back golden leather drapes and entered a softly lit, almost perfectly octagonal chamber about fifty feet across and of indeterminate height. The floor was of granite blocks set in cement no thicker than a sheet of paper. The ceiling, almost obscured by the gloom, was supported by thick upright pillars, which rose in parallel lines from the floor. The walls were of magnesia veined with talc. In the exact center of the room

Descent into The Chasm

hung a giant fire opal.

It was pear-shaped, big as a bushel basket and was suspended from the ceiling by a single silver chain. The movement of air caused by Ozma's entry started the opal to turn slowly. As it turned it picked up the rays of light from the wall lamps and reflected them back in flowing hues of blue and pink and yellow and green opalescent fire. Ozma approached the opal and was soon enveloped in its warm glow. In its gentle heat her body tingled and shivered deliciously, as one's body does when one comes from a cold place into warm sunshine. Ozma took off her cap and shook free her hair until it fell in a golden waterfall over her shoulders. She looked at her hands and found that all the burns and blisters had disappeared and that the soreness had gone out of her muscles.

Ozma peered deep into the translucent depths of the fire opal and saw images almost without form — like thoughts caught up in amber — appearing and disappearing like dancers in some mysterious ballet. The dance seemed to be nearly always gay and sparkling, with only occasional somber overtones. It continued on for several minutes and then without warning the dance stopped and Ozma could see only the ever changing surface colors of the opal.

Descent into The Chasm

She turned away and walked down the lane of stone pillars until she came to a foot thick door which swung wide as she approached and closed behind her with an almost inaudible thud as she entered the room.

This room was of medium size, with porphyry and granite walls which had been hand rubbed to a marble-like smoothness. One side wall was embellished with silver inlay and the other with gold. The front and rear walls were of their natural beauty. The chamber was lighted by the soft glow of lamps set into the walls and there was a faint odor of incense, fragrant and soothing, curling from the jeweled censers.

There was a woman sitting at a carved wood and ivory table, set back from the center of the room. She was of indefinite age with soft brown hair and brown eyes that shone like the eyes of an eagle. Her hands, unwrinkled, with long slender fingers lay motionless on the otherwise completely bare table top. She was dressed in a gown of linen and silk, snow white and so ample that its folds were like carvings in stone. Over her hair and falling free to the floor was a heliotrope colored scarf. There was no other color and the woman wore no jewelry. She looked at Ozma for a long moment.

"You are welcome, my dear," she said. "If I may be so presumptuous as to welcome the ruler of OZ to a place in her own realm. Please be seated and allow me to introduce myself. I am Lurline."

Her voice, even though calm and restrained, rang as a struck silver bell and the tones seemed to linger in the air even after she had stopped speaking.

Ozma felt a chair touch the back of her legs and she sat down, a little awed by the presence of this mighty fairy queen. 'So this is Queen Lurline,' she thought. 'This is the Presence referred to by the Voice of the Hill.'

"Welcome to the Land of OZ, Queen Lurline," Ozma said aloud, and then asked, "How can I be of service to you?"

It is noted in the Fairy Archives that Lurline is Queen of the Trooping Fairies and that her powers overshadow even those of the Great Djinn,

214

Descent into The Chasm

Tititi-Hoochoo. Queen Lurline is described as the one who came to OZ when it was an ordinary country and transformed it, together with all its people, its animals and even its plants, into an enchantingly beautiful fairyland. Queen Lurline now lives in the Forest of Burzee, a land to the south of Rosewood Meadows and on the other side of the Great Sandy Waste from OZ. This waste is part of the Deadly Desert which entirely surrounds the Land of OZ. It was to the Forest of Burzee that the dryad, Lark Ellen, and her retinue of hamadryads retired when they left the Forest of the Fighting Trees.

Now that Ozma was seated at the table Lurline looked at her closely, thanked her for her welcome and said, "I hope I may be of service to you and that we may become fast friends, Princess."

Then she added, smilingly, "Your clothes are strange garb for a princess, but they did serve their purpose by disguising your true identity and allowing you access to things which might have been denied you had people recognized you at once as their ruler. But however well clothes disguise a body they can seldom disguise the goodness contained in that body. Polychrome knew at once that you were no wandering boy, as did several others you met. And these meetings occurred before the OPALOZ had worked its charm on your scratched face and blistered hands. But I think that by now you have decided to discard the camouflage and remain a girl, bending your energies toward the betterment of your land and your people."

Ozma agreed.

"This has been a wonderful adventure but now I think that I am ready to settle down and rule. The next time I go adventuring, if ever, it will be as Princess Ozma, not as Tip.

"Lurline, please tell me about that tremendous fire opal in the outer chamber. You called it the OPALOZ. What is it? Who brought it? What is the magic it performs?" begged Ozma.

"The OPALOZ works no magic," began Lurline, "but it helps to allow certain selected persons to look into their essential natures and see a perfect body. It can aid in healing the flesh, but it can only reflect the spirit. It does have power, though; you felt that power and you saw it, too. You felt its energy and life giving force coursing through your body, healing your burns and blisters and soothing the ache in your muscles. It does the same thing for the Land of OZ. I brought the OPALOZ here and set it in place inside this hill and I ordered the Hammerheads to guard it. Their orders are to allow no one access without authority and you saw how well they carried out their duties, perhaps a little too eagerly. The Voice of the Hill is here to supervise the activities of the Hammerheads.

"As long as the OPALOZ is in place this land will be blessed by the goodness and light which emanates from it. If it were ever to be destroyed or removed, OZ would again become just an ordinary country, subject to the disappointments, unhappiness and jealousies that other places have.

"You must think good thoughts, do good deeds and reflect good images. If you need help to help yourself, you need only ask. But before you can expect to receive help you must use all the will you have. Use your will and watch it grow, for competence comes from understanding and understanding can be gained only by constant practice. If you can truly say: I will always help anyone who asks my aid – without expectation of reward; I will never maliciously harm anyone or anything; I will never betray a trust, and I will give love to all – no matter what is returned, and if you constantly practice these tenets then you will have a good base for beginning to understand wisdom.

"In your trials, and you will have many of them, if you keep your ideals you will find that help will come to you from the most unexpected quarters. Suggestions and actions, which sometimes appear ridiculous, will many times solve a problem. But none of these plans may be violent. Violence breeds only violence and it never solves a problem. Help will come to you because of what you know and what you practice; it will not come merely by coincidence.

"In closing, Ozma, you realize I am sure that the location and even the fact that the OPALOZ is in the Land of OZ must be kept a tightly held secret. To this end you should come here only when all else has failed and OZ, not you, faces complete disaster. You are unimportant. OZ must be preserved. In this regard you must realize that the OPALOZ cannot solve your problems for you. It can only assist you by refreshing your consciousness thus allowing your mind free rein to reason out your difficulties. Remember always to wear a primrose when you come here, otherwise you will not be admitted. Without the primrose you will not be able to descend that set of steps.

"Enough of that, Ozma, let us talk about you and Glinda and that marvelous little Sawhorse of yours. He is priceless and that knotty head of his seems to contain all the wisdom of the oaks and much of that of the dryads. His finest quality, though, is his unswerving loyalty and devotion to you."

So the two sat for some time discussing many things: the goodness of Glinda; the love of Jellia Jamb; of who could come — and how — to the Land of OZ, and of what is meant by 'dominion over all.' Then in mutual cognizance they realized that the time had come for them to part, and Lurline said .

"Please give Glinda my love and tell her that you met and spoke with me here under this hill."

"May I tell Glinda of the OPALOZ?"

"She knows," replied Lurline, "and there are two others in OZ who know." She whispered their names to Ozma.

With that Lurline stood, kissed Ozma and said, "Give me both your hands, my dear, and close your eyes."

When Ozma opened her eyes, she was standing alone beside the leg of the dolmen at the end of the hawthorn bordered path. At her side stood the faithful Sawhorse and the intact Red Wagon. She climbed quietly into the conveyance and asked the Sawhorse to take her to Glinda's palace. The Sawhorse, ever considerate of her feelings, made his way wordlessly down the hill.

Chapter 20

Glinda's Palace

or the last time Ozma and the Sawhorse rejoined the pink oyster shell road and they were not to leave that road again until they arrived at the gates of Glinda's palace. Through the fields carpeted with moist, green grass, over gentle slopes and through otherwise pathless valleys the Sawhorse drew the sparkling Red Wagon. The Sawhorse's footfalls were muffled by the soft texture of the crushed oyster shells, and the wheels of the Red Wagon skimmed lightly and soundlessly over the road.

The pale evening, now, was all around them. A huge silver moon, hanging low on the eastern horizon, shone coldly. The sun had sunk in the west and the sky there was only slightly roseate. The fragrant lightness of these May evenings in OZ is amazing; good fortune and happiness must spring from the very same source as does the gentleness of this weather.

They rode past scattered houses, crimson with bouganvilla and point-settia, some of whose occupants were sitting on their front porches enjoy-

219

Glinda's Palace

ing the calm of this, the most restful time of day. Many waved greetings to the young 'boy' in his Red Wagon drawn by the strange wooden creature and wished him well.

They were nearing Glinda's palace now. Its many domes and pinnacles glimmered with a soft whiteness, but the granite and porphyry walls blushed rose-red in the sunset. The Sawhorse trotted up to the high arched gate, fitted with two heavy doors, and waited while Ozma alighted and walked to the gate. On one door was a ruby knocker fitted to strike on a plaque of the finest gold. Ozma thumped three times slowly, paused, then rapped once.

Glinda's Palace

The doors opened into an entry yard, walled and paved with red marble. A uniformed sentry stepped forward, saluted and said .

"In the name of Glinda, Royal Sorceress of OZ, Good Witch of the South, Ruler of Rosewood Meadows — the land of the Quadling people — Greetings and Welcome, Your Majesty. I am your escort, Captain Belle."

"Thank you, Captain. I have come to see Glinda the Good. Will you take me to her, please?" asked Ozma.

"With pleasure, Princess Ozma," said the girl captain. "May I accompany you in your conveyance? I have never ridden in such a beautiful wagon, drawn by such a remarkable creature."

This young woman was an officer in the army of Glinda the Good. This army is unusual because it is made up entirely of girls. This is not to say, however, that it is not effective, quite the contrary. These soldier girls wear gay and pretty uniforms and are equipped with long and glistening silver tipped spears, the shafts of which are inlaid with mother-of-pearl. All the officers have sharp, gleaming swords and their shields are edged with peacock feathers. Altogether they form a brilliant army, well trained, well disciplined and effective.

This army had been organized by Glinda before Ozma took her rightful place as ruler of all OZ and at that time had been used as a counterweight against several wicked witches who inhabited OZ. Now that Ozma was queen the army was relegated to a more or less ceremonial status. But Glinda still felt that it was a good idea to have an army trained and ready to fight. In that way if all other methods to defeat an enemy — should one appear — fail, the army could be used if Ozma so desired. The girls who constituted this army came from all parts of the Land of OZ, and all were volunteers who considered it a great honor and privilege to serve Glinda.

221

Glinda's Palace

Twilight had almost failed as the group passed through a garden of grape arbors and melon vines, with date palms spaced at regular intervals. The gold shod hooves of the Sawhorse rang out as he drew the Red Wagon and its passengers over the multi-colored marble walks which led through the palace grounds. The beauty of these grounds with their superb shrubs, fragrant flowers and shade and fruit trees, could not be really appreciated in the gathering gloom of evening. But even though their color was muted by the night, nothing could disguise the fragrance of a peach orchard's candy sweet, pink blossoms. Then they arrived at the steps of Glinda's palace and Glinda met them there.

She wore only a simple white gown, but that night in honor of Ozma her dress absolutely glittered with gems. Her auburn hair was studded with diamonds and around her neck she wore a necklace of diamonds and sapphires mixed. The blue of the sapphires accentuated the brilliance of her deep blue eyes. She had never been dressed more splendidly, nor had she ever before looked younger or more beautiful. A little distance behind her stood Ozma's maid, friend and confidant—Jellia Jamb.

Ozma, even though conscious of her grimy and dishevelled appearance—in spite of the action of the OPALOZ—was overjoyed to see both her dearest friends waiting to greet her. Oh! the hugs and kisses. Oh! the tears of joy and happiness at this reunion. And the greetings and the questions and the answers as they all seemingly talked at once, as is the habit and custom of all women in times of joy or stress.

Glinda's Palace

Then arm in arm the three of them tripped and swirled into a small nook where a dinner for three was served. Ozma was hungry and Glinda and Jellia Jamb, now that the anxiety caused by Ozma's disappearance was over, ate as though they were famished.

At no time during or after the dinner did either Glinda or Jellia Jamb have the lack of consideration or understanding to chide Ozma for having worried them by her unannounced departure. They knew that she would realize, if she had not already realized, the pain and anguish they had been through and that she would never again subject them to this worry.

Dinner over, the three went across the hall into the Crimson Room, one of the many sitting rooms in Glinda's palace. It is a striking room and well named for it is carpeted in crimson, has crimson colored chairs and tables and long, comfortable velvet sofas with heavily carved and gilded frames. Large wall mirrors of a type no longer made, not even in the Land of OZ, are interspersed with sumptuous tapestries. The room has a butter colored ceiling, bordered with red gold, from which a shower of crystal hangs, shimmering and sparkling in the soft light of many tapers.

There on a table awaiting Ozma was a gift from Tititi-Hoochoo, the Great Djinn. With his dragonel safely returned, Tititi-Hoochoo had kept the promise he had made to himself and had sent Ozma a picture. Glinda handed it to her and said:

"Ozma, dear, have you ever seen anything as beautiful as these wrappings?"

Ozma had not, nor had anyone else, ever. For the package was wrapped in color. There was no paper, no cloth, no string or cord. The picture was wrapped in an opaque emerald green color with ribbons and bows of daffodil yellow binding it. Ozma undid the color ribbons, smoothed out the color wrapping, and disclosed a picture. A magic picture, undoubtedly, although now it only showed a rather pretty rural scene.

Ozma turned the picture over, curiously, and saw a note attached

to the back which read, "If
you wish to see any one or
anyplace, you need only
express the wish and the
desired scene will appear in
the picture."

Ozma, Glinda and Jellia
took turns asking to see various places and people and,
sure enough, as soon as the
request was made the scene
was shown. After the scene
had appeared for a few moments it faded from view and
was replaced by the original
painting.

"Ooh!" exclaimed Ozma,
"This is wonderful. I will hang
it in my boudoir and then if I
ever want to know where anyone is all I have to do is ask.

"I must send a message of thanks to the Great Djinn for this lovely
gift and those magnificent wrappings as soon as I get back to Emerald City,"

"If we had only had the Magic Picture when Ozma was first kidnapped, we could have found her much quicker than we did," said Jellia
Jamb to Glinda.

"That is very true," Glinda replied, "But if it had not been for you,
Jellia, I don't think we ever would have found out what the Wizard and
Mombi had done with her in the first place."

Jellia Jamb blushed with pride and happiness at this recognition of
her accomplishment. Glinda continued,

"I also remember that I had some difficulty in convincing Ozma to discard 'Tip' and resume her rightful body. Among other things 'Tip' grumbled that he did not want to have to wear "all those girl's dresses and things all the time," and that girls never have any fun or adventures. But Tip finally agreed and it looks to me that 'he' made the right decision for I see one girl who is not wearing "those pretty dresses" and has certainly had a very adventurous time. But in any event the ceremony was held. Do you remember it?"

They all sat in silence for a few moments reliving that memorable event.

Glinda had finally captured Mombi and had promised that no harm would come to her if she would promise to give up witchcraft after performing one more act of magical transformation under Glinda's supervision. This was to return Ozma to her proper body.

Mombi reluctantly agreed, and at the designated time and place in the palace grounds, she gave Tip a potion. He drank it and immediately fell into a deep sleep. He was placed on a couch which was piled high with cushions and draped with hangings which effectively hid him from view.

Glinda's Palace

Then evil old Mombi spread out many weird and mysterious tools of witchcraft and magic upon the ground. After arranging them in the exact positions prescribed by the Encyclopedia of Magic, she began to murmur the preparatory incantations. She made several passes with her hands over the small vases and vials which were bubbling obscenely. She then placed both hands over a silver bowl, the contents of which were foaming violently, uttered one magic word and scattered a handful of herbs into the bowl. There was a flash and a thick violet cloud filled the air. Mombi chanted seven more phrases and the air cleared.

Glinda's Palace

As soon as the assembled people were able to see again, Glinda went to the draped couch and parted the hangings. Out stepped a young girl — fresh and beautiful as a May morning. Her eyes sparkled as twin diamonds and her lips were tinted like a tourmaline. A splendid jeweled circlet confined her golden tresses. Her outer dress of Michelin floated over her satin slip like a cloud, and dainty satin slippers shod her feet.

Glinda's Palace

Coming out of her reverie with a sigh, Glinda said.

"She was the most beautiful sight I have ever seen, but look at her now. Please, Ozma, please, as soon as you arrive at Emerald City throw those ridiculous boy's clothes away and in the future wear things more becoming to a beautiful girl and more appropriate to the Ruler of Oz.

"Now, I am going to send both of you back to Emerald City in my sky chariot for I know Ozma must be exhausted. So kiss me good-bye."

Ozma kissed her and together with her loyal handmaiden got into the stork drawn chariot and set out into the night sky.

Chapter 21

Home Again

urple Ozian night. Night set with a million twinkling stars. The full moon, riding high in the sky — round, demure and frosty — poured her light over the countryside below, while it also silvered the unique sky chariot.

The chariot was large enough to carry six passengers comfortably, and was strong enough to carry them safely. It was high in the back and low in the front and looked something like a toboggan. On the blunt prow was a dragon painted in twenty colors and on each side was Glinda's monogram, intertwined with mistletoe and Cecile Bruner rose buds. There was also a canopy of some crimson material embroidered with gold dragons to ward off the direct rays of the sun. As it was not used at night the canopy was furled and stowed in a locker at the rear of the chariot.

Ozma and Jellia Jamb were lounging comfortably in the fore part of the craft, when Jellia spoke:

"Ozma, I asked the Sawhorse to please bring your Red Wagon back

to Emerald City, and he said that he would bring it tonight. When I asked him if he intended to swim the Chad River, he looked at me in that strange manner of his and snorted. So I teased him and said that the ferryman would make him chop wood before he would row him and the Red Wagon across the river, and do you know what he said? He said, 'Humph, now that I have the royal insigne of OZ on my Red Wagon, I dare any boatman not to give me passage — night or day!'

"Did you catch his reference to 'MY' Red Wagon? He has already taken possession of it."

Ozma laughed and said, "I am not worried about the Sawhorse bringing the Red Wagon to Emerald City, but I suppose I should be concerned about the ferryman's toes if he is too nasty to the Sawhorse. As for ownership of the Red Wagon, it is as much his as mine and I am glad that he enjoys having it."

Then soothed by the beat of nine pairs of powerful wings in the soft cool of the night the two girls fell silent, each wrapped in her own thoughts.

"I can't help comparing this chariot to the Gump. Remember him, Jellia?" asked Ozma, breaking the silence.

Jellia certainly did and could not help smiling to herself as she remembered that astonishing creation. The Gump was a product of a committee's thinking. It had been put together by Tip, the Scarecrow, the Tin Woodman, Jack Pumpkinhead and the Woggle-Bug so that they could all fly away from Emerald City which was being beseiged by General Jinjur's army. The Gump was made up of two highbacked sofas — bound together with clothesline, four palm fronds to serve as wings, a broom for a tail, and the antlered head of a strange beast known as a Gump. Tip then brought it to life with the same Powder of Life he had used on the Sawhorse. The Gump flew, not comfortably, but it flew.

Again the girls sat wrapped in their own thoughts, with Ozma reflecting on her meeting with Queen Lurline. She pondered the explanation Lurline had given for one of the most perplexing anomalies of OZ.

Lurline had told her that in order to avoid overcrowding, not everyone who desired to come to OZ could be accomodated. Before an outsider could even be considered for entrance into OZ someone in OZ would have to leave and seek adventures in another place. Then an outsider would be selected to come to OZ at whatever age that person selected. In OZ the selectee could remain a child, teenager, adult or oldster for as many years as he or she would be happy. Then, when that person had learned what he had come to OZ to learn, he or she could ask to be allowed to leave.

This aging process also applied to those who were living in OZ at the time it was enchanted. Most of those people are good but some, unfortunately, have retained some of their old faults and so they may not leave OZ until most if not all of their faults have been corrected.

"This applies to all but you, Ozma," Lurline had said. "You were selected to be the girl ruler of OZ and when you reach your predetermined age, you will remain that age until you have completed your mission in OZ."

As Ozma pondered this revelation a sudden thought struck her. If the only way anyone could come to OZ was by means of Lurline's selection plan, how could one account for the Wizard and Dorothy Gale being able to enter? Were accidental arrivals the exception? But if accidents were the only exceptions, how about Mr. Wainwright's planned entry from Ev? Ozma shook her head in perplexity and decided to ask Glinda for the answer, if Glinda knew.

Jellia nudged Ozma and whispered, "Did you notice how awkward the stork maidens seem to be when they are on the ground in their costumes, with those long bills and the very deliberate way they lift those stilty legs of theirs to walk? But when they are flying, with those long bills outthrust and the long legs trailing behind, they are the picture of streamlined grace."

"Yes, I noticed," answered Ozma, "and they pull the chariot so effortlessly that other than the whisper of the wind as it flows by the chariot, their passage through the sky is almost noiseless."

As they flew on Ozma thought of what Glinda had told her when they discussed the subject of Ozma's duties as ruler. Glinda said that for many years she had acted as regent for Ozma and had selected those who would come to OZ.

"It is not an easy task as you will soon discover," Glinda had told her. "For although only three or four people a day can be selected, many must be screened and great care taken in the final determination. I select only those whose presence I feel will benefit all the land. This does not mean that they must be perfect, because perfection in itself does not mean happiness. But because OZ is a happy land the people selected to come to OZ must be happy ones and must have the ability to make others happy.

"I judge those who want to come to OZ by their actions and behavior rather than by pleas and importunities. I select people of all ages, including children, for admittance, for age is of no concern in OZ — as Lurline explained to you. The prime requisite, of course, is the desire to come to OZ. Some of those fortunate enough to be selected will come to OZ at once, while others may be selected many years before they come. The manner by which you choose will be entirely your own, and as soon as you feel able to begin making the selections I will be happy to turn this task over to you," Glinda had concluded.

Over the quiet landscape the sky chariot flew until in the distance the spires and turrets of Emerald City began to take shape. Jellia Jamb, who was thirsty, poured out two glasses of Ozade and both girls drank.

Ozma thanked her and said, "As much as I like Ozade, I like ice cream sodas better, and first thing tomorrow morning I am going to have

a free public ice cream soda fountain built so that everyone can have all the ice cream sodas they want."

The sky chariot was now sweeping low over the sleeping Emerald City as Ozma pointed and exclaimed:

"Look there, Jellia, right at that corner. That is where I will have the soda fountain built."

The sky chariot circled the royal palace once and then settled down gently in Ozma's rose garden. Ozma thanked the leader of the stork maidens for the lovely trip and then she and Jellia Jamb watched the beautiful chariot rise smoothly and silently and sail southward toward Glinda's palace.

As the two girls entered the palace and passed through the great hallway, the head of the Gump, mounted over the mantel of the massive fireplace, opened its eyes, waggled its saucy chin whiskers and called out:

"Good night, Jellia. You are up awfully late for so young a girl. Say good night to your friend for me and sleep tight."

The two girls answered his greeting and made their way quietly up the great staircase to Ozma's suite of rooms. As she tucked Ozma into her big comfortable bed, Jellia assured Ozma that she would search out the Scarecrow and tell him of Ozma's safe return.

Ozma snuggled down happily but sleepily and wriggled her toes. And then, just as she was falling asleep, she thought of the four people — a grown man and woman and a little girl and boy — who had been selected that very day by Glinda to come to OZ at the proper time.

She wondered when she would meet them and what they would be like, these four happy, but unknowing people who were to come to the Marvelous Land of OZ.

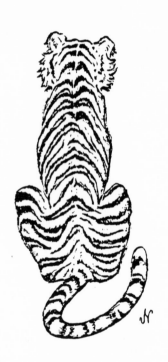